Donald MacKenzie and The Murder Room

>>> This title is part of The Murder Room, our series dedicated to making available out-of-print or hard-to-find titles by classic crime writers.

Crime fiction has always held up a mirror to society. The Victorians were fascinated by sensational murder and the emerging science of detection; now we are obsessed with the forensic detail of violent death. And no other genre has so captivated and enthralled readers.

Vast troves of classic crime writing have for a long time been unavailable to all but the most dedicated frequenters of second-hand bookshops. The advent of digital publishing means that we are now able to bring you the backlists of a huge range of titles by classic and contemporary crime writers, some of which have been out of print for decades.

From the genteel amateur private eyes of the Golden Age and the femmes fatales of pulp fiction, to the morally ambiguous hard-boiled detectives of mid twentieth-century America and their descendants who walk our twenty-first century streets, The Murder Room has it all. **>>>**

The Murder Room
Where Criminal Minds Meet

themurderroom.com

T0352219

Donald MacKenzie 1908–1994

Donald MacKenzie was born in Ontario, Canada, and educated in England, Canada and Switzerland. For twenty-five years MacKenzie lived by crime in many countries. 'I went to jail,' he wrote, 'if not with depressing regularity, too often for my liking.' His last sentences were five years in the United States and three years in England, running consecutively. He began writing and selling stories when in American jail. 'I try to do exactly as I like as often as possible and I don't think I'm either psychopathic, a wayward boy, a problem of our time, a charming rogue. Or ever was.'

He had a wife, Estrela, and a daughter, and they divided their time between England, Portugal, Spain and Austria.

The Genial Stranger

Donald MacKenzie

An Orion book

Copyright © The Estate of Donald MacKenzie 1962

The right of Donald MacKenzie to be identified as the author of this work has
been asserted in accordance with the Copyright, Designs and Patents Act 1988.

This edition published by
The Orion Publishing Group Ltd
Orion House
5 Upper St Martin's Lane
London WC2H 9EA

An Hachette UK company
A CIP catalogue record for this book is available from the British Library

ISBN 978 1 4719 0569 8

www.orionbooks.co.uk

A book for Judy Russell marking a friendship that has always been hard for others to understand.

BEWARE OF THE GENIAL STRANGER!

Confidence tricksters are operating throughout Europe. Be on your guard against the man wanting to reward you for returning his dropped wallet—the self-styled doctor, judge or stockbroker introduced by some new acquaintance.

Confidence-tricksters play on greed and vanity. Their methods are skilled and varied, their poses often difficult of detection.

Before parting with money to strangers on ANY pretext, check with your banker or with the local police.

A notice displayed in banks and travel agencies.

CHAPTER I

TUESDAY A.M.

AT BROMPTON ROAD, Russell used a shoulder to fight his way off the crowded bus. Sound of a striking clock lingered as he turned into the quiet square. In front of him, the Victorian façade of an apartment building warmed in the early-morning sunshine. He went up the steps.

Inside, a faded carpet covered the entrance hall. Two forbidding busts guarded the central stairway. A porter moved rheumatically from the shadows. Seeing Russell, he blinked recognition. A row of campaign ribbons brightened the man's high-necked uniform. The jet of his waxed moustache was made suspect by thinning grey hair.

Russell followed him as far as the ancient elevator. The porter hauled on the handrope, grumbling his way to the top floor. He threw open the cage door, thrusting a couple of newspapers at the Canadian.

" The paper bill's inside, sir. Per'aps you'd tell Mr. Sergeant the boy's been about it. *Twice !* " He slammed the cage shut.

Sergeant's door was at the far end of the building. For a moment, Russell stood in front of it listening. No sound came from inside. He pushed his fingers under the mail flap, rapped it three times. No one answered. Now he bent down, holding the spring-loaded flap and calling through it. A smell of burning fat drifted up his nose.

The catch was lifted cautiously. No more than Sergeant's head showed. He retreated, widening the gap in the door. When he had let Russell in, he stood with his back to the door. Sergeant was a short man with white hair, dressed in a woollen bathrobe. His burned-sugar voice was reproving.

1

" What happened to you, Gordy ? Didn't you get my message ? "

Russell added the newspapers to a pile of unopened bills on the chest in the hall. He took a close look at the other's plump unshaven face—the egg festooning the lapels of the bathrobe.

" I got all three of your messages," he said at last and led the way into the high-ceilinged living-room. He jerked down the window, rattling the frame in its runners. Children were already at play in the railed gardens below. Russell turned slowly. The remains of his partner's breakfast littered the table. Through the open doorway, a jumble of blankets trailed from the bed. Fat smoked in some forgotten frying-pan out in the kitchen.

Russell trailed the stench, threw a switch and came back to take a chair. He avoided Sergeant's glare of disapproval, concerned about his own expression. Paul would be touchy. This bore all the earmarks of being one of those mornings. The messy feeding, unshaven face and total disorder. At this moment, imaginary death, doom and disaster would be rattling round inside Paul's head. It was hardly the moment to hit him with news of real trouble. Nor did the necessity of doing it ease the situation.

Sergeant was padding from wall to wall, his fat bare calves thrust into jazzy-patterned slipsocks. He thrust out both arms as he made the turn, the wings of white hair over his ears agitated with the movement.

" Suppose you tell me what sort of hours you keep ! I've been trying to reach you since eight o'clock last night ! "

Russell studied the tips of his black brogues, controlling his temper. At times like this, it was as well to remember the first occasion on which he'd seen Sergeant. Even now, the recollection was uncomfortable. The self-acclaimed boy-wonder who'd landed at Cherbourg, God knows how many years ago. Back in those days, the mob used to hang out in a bar behind the Continentale in Paris. It was an address that had been given to him. He still recalled the ring of hostile faces that had stared down his entrance. It

2

was Sergeant who had picked him out of a crummy walk-up on the Left Bank—Sergeant who had staked him and taught him how to steer a mark with the best of them.

" *Sergeant's lance-corporal!* " The nickname the mob had hung on him both admitted and classified the Canadian.

Loyalty was something thieves took for granted. At least, con-men did. Without it, you were dead. What they would never know was how much deeper his feeling for this old man went.

Russell forced himself to look up across the table. He spoke quietly. " I didn't use this phone because you told me there was a tap on it. Brace gave me a pull last night, Paul. I was in Bow Street Station till one o'clock this morning."

Sergeant fumbled a cigar from a package. He continued to hold the wrong end to the flame till the younger man reversed it for him. Sergeant spread his weight in a chair, fighting an early smoker's bark. He wiped the corners of his eyes with a sleeve and waited.

Russell continued, standing at the window, broad-shouldered in grey tweeds. " Maybe you wouldn't call it a pinch—just a pull under the Old Pal's Act. Detective-Sergeant Joe Brace and another joker from the Yard. We've been credited with the Beasley score, Paul. Laugh *that* off! I didn't bother trying to put Brace straight. He's quite happy with the theory. He wants fifty pounds by to-night or else. ' Even a cop has to live.' I quote the bastard! "

Sergeant's cigar hissed in an empty coffee cup. " The hell with Brace," he said hollowly. " I've got worse trouble than that. A helluva lot worse! I need your help, Gordy! "

Russell grinned his appreciation of the old man's artistry. He knew every line of every role Sergeant played. The frantic calls to Russell's hotel last night suggested some sort of major production. The dropped egg and disorder added probability. This stirring appeal for help left no doubt. The only question was how the sandbag would be wielded. Russell's voice was patient.

" Not even if you've got a horse going in a heat by

himself, Paul. There's nothing left—NOTHING ! I've got a bridge hand in pawn tickets—there's nothing left I could raise a fiver on. I'm going to tell you something. We've got to get out and hustle, as of now. Even if it means playing the Seat ! "

He waited for the shocked rolling periods. *The Seat! Listen, my boy! Thirty years, I've been handling the public. When the time comes that I've got to ask a mark to believe that sort of crap—tie me to a lamp-post!*

It wasn't true, of course. Yet all oldtimers set up this squawk before using the con-man's standby for eating money. The Hot Seat was a crude but effective ploy. And the fact remained that it was four months since he and Sergeant had earned a nickel.

He looked up at his partner. Sergeant was standing quite still, his face expressionless.

"We need that fifty to-night," urged Russell. " Brace is hostile. He's convinced he's on the wrong end of a swindle."

Sergeant's hands turned in a gesture of despair beyond acting. He sat down, gripping the edge of the table. Russell took the cable form. It was a long time before the pattern of printed words made sense to him.

ARRIVE LONDON WEDNESDAY PANAMERICAN FLIGHT 703
LOVE LUCY

He creased and recreased the form between nervous fingers. As long as he remembered, Sergeant had been expending money and emotion on a daughter he'd seen three times in twenty years. The last occasion was a decade ago. For what must have been the girl's entire lifetime, Sergeant had managed to produce a myth of success and respectability for her. The facts were hard to determine—the old man never talked of his ex-wife. Whether or not she knew the score, she seemed to have kept Sergeant's halo brightly burnished. The girl and her mother lived in California. As long as there was a Federal Government,

4

Sergeant would never put a foot back in the United States. It was all too easy, thought Russell. As far as Mrs. Sergeant was concerned, her husband could call himself a minister of the gospel. If he kept paying the bills.

Russell's mouth was derisory. " This is all we needed. Miss California on the strength. What's her angle this time ? "

Sergeant turned from the window, red-faced and aggressive. " You can cut that out—you don't talk about angles with Lucy ! " He deflated as suddenly. " For God's sake, Gordy—I just don't know."

Russell walked to the kitchen. By the time he was back with the bubbling percolator, Sergeant had shaved and dressed. Sunlight invaded the shabby room, searching the dusty floor, the broken-backed furniture. He poured the coffee, his voice gentle.

" I'm sorry, Paul. What are we going to do about her ? "

Sergeant's fine blue suiting was cut artfully to conceal the bulge in his middle. His smooth white hair bore a gloss.

" God knows ! I can think of nothing else but trying to stop her. If not . . . "

Russell looked at him curiously. It was a crazy thing—if you applied society's tests to this old thief, you could fault him every time. Yet Russell had never known a man who was less hypocritical. No one whose integrity—at least on one plane—was greater.

" She must have given you some sort of hint in a letter," he persisted. Already he knew the answer—too long had he suffered those gassy schoolgirl scrawls. True—the last three years had brought a more intelligent appreciation of the completely fictitious life invented for himself by her father. Each letter was read aloud to Russell. Never could there be any criticism—even implicit. A hundred times, Russell had wanted to shock his partner out of his complacency—it touched the stark business of stealing a living with lunacy. Letters, letters and letters, mailed with dispatch from father to daughter and back again. The long hauls to a series of American Express offices in as many cities. Broke or in the money, the first call always had to be for Lucy's mail. This past year or so, even the need to get hold of cash seemed to escape Sergeant. Provided he was six months ahead on the money that supported his daughter, nothing else seemed to matter.

" Think ! " urged Russell. " There must be something she said that would give us a clue." The under-pinnings of Sergeant's world were slipping. Russell's secret satisfaction was tinged with guilt.

" I've tried thinking back—there's nothing. If I knew the girl it might be easier. The truth is, I don't even know my own daughter." Sergeant shook his head, a fat bewildered old man. " Wednesday. If I can't get in touch with her, she'll be here on our doorstep."

Russell looked up, remembering the unpaid bills in the hall, the sheaf of pawn tickets at his hotel. This was no time to pull punches. He waved a hand round the shabby apartment.

" She's going to get a shock. The big company promoter ! " he said sarcastically. " This time, you got stuck with your own production, Paul. Suppose we forget about Lucy for a moment. Brace wasn't kidding about that fifty quid. To-night, he said. He meant it ! "

Sergeant brushed a speck from his lapel, his expression suddenly tranquil. " Screw Brace," he said with composure. " I'm not knocking at the knees every time some lousy cop tries a shakedown. I'm not stopping Lucy, boy. I think she needs me." Russell climbed on his feet. By now, he knew when argument was useless. " Whatever you say, Paul. All we need is four or five hundred quid to put up a front for her. You better wave a wand."

Sergeant sat down at the table, carefully avoiding the mess he had made previously.

" We've got to be careful, Gordy. After all these years, hearing about you, Lucy'll have very definite ideas about what to expect."

The Canadian's smile was mocking. " You bet she will ! The clean-cut Brooks Brothers type—personal assistant to

the Big Man himself. And the loot to put all this over ? "
He rubbed a finger against thumb.

Sergeant's manner was confident. " Ah—we'll get it.
We're not going to need as much as you think—Lucy won't
be here that long. We can do it on two hundred and fifty.
Little Arthur Ryan's our man—the bum's been trying to
lend me money for twenty years. And he's got it to lend.
Now listen . . ." His voice was assured as he added logic to
grafter's sense and tied the package neatly before giving it
to Russell.

The younger man was only half-convinced. " I'll try
him for you, Paul, but I don't think he'll go for it myself.
When did Ryan ever relinquish a buck he didn't think would
make two ? It isn't *his* daughter, remember. The only
female Ryan ever got worked up about was Mumtaz Mahal
—when she got beat, he gave it up. You want to forget this
mania for the truth, Pop. You need the money. Let me
tell Ryan that we've got a mark lined up—we need the dough
for expenses."

Sergeant shook his head obstinately. " I keep my pitch
for the mugs, Gordy. Not our own kind. You make Little
Arthur sound a tougher proposition than he really is—he'll
lend us the money." He crossed the room, lifted the telephone receiver, listened and then replaced it. " I want to
know as soon as you've got that money—I'll tell you what
to do. Dial this number—let the bell ring twice then hang
up. That'll be my signal. If these bums still have a tap on
this thing, it'll give 'em something to think about."

By the time Russell reached Rifkind's, the long sandwich-
bar was crowded. The neighbourhood noon-hour trade
was predominately male. A few Jewish tailors ; the staff
from the fight-promoter's office ; tired chorus-boys from
the next-door rehearsal rooms. The con-mob had been
using the place for the last couple of years. Three tables at
the end of the room and out of sight always bore the
RESERVED sign. Sam Rifkind served good food and minded
nobody's business but his own.

7

He looked up at Russell, his face the colour of the hot salt beef he was slicing; "Mr. Ryan—yes, back there!" He pointed a knife honed to a sliver. His metallic voice was pitched to cut through a chef's bawling, the whine of the Gaggia coffee-machine.

Little Arthur's table was covered with plates. He paused in the business of spearing chopped liver long enough to register Russell's arrival. The Australian ate in dedicated fashion, his quick dark eyes scanning Russell. Little Arthur had the strong hands and wrists of an ex-jockey and used a double-up cushion to give himself height.

Russell waited; remembering Little Arthur's insistence on protocol. Time and again, Russell had felt like hanging the tiny Australian on some clothes hook, walking away and leaving him there kicking. But Ryan was a power. Ten years ago, he had parlayed a half-dozen coups into a sizeable fortune and retired as an active thief. Over the past few years he identified himself with some sort of Elder Statesman. He was busy with unsought advice—a hairbag whose reminiscences were tolerated for one reason. Little Arthur's money financed half the con-men in Europe. He was ready to put up expenses against return of his outlay plus twenty per cent of the take. If Ryan had ever been guilty of pure charity, Russell had not heard about it.

Little Arthur swabbed his mouth free of grease. He had a tough Sydney accent and an aggressive delivery.

"Gawdblimey, sport! I heard you were in the nick—that Brace had taken you in!"

Russell took a chair uninvited. Ryan only bought meals for people who didn't need them.

"That's right. I was in. Now I'm out. Sergeant's asked me to come and see you, Arthur."

Little Arthur used a fistful of cold chicken as a buffer. He considered the implications of the statement then answered ponderously.

"Did he, now! Well—it's about time he got off his arse and stopped living in the past. The game's changed, Gordy. Mugs don't come to you—you've got to get out

8

and find 'em. I suppose he wants front money—is that it? "

The context of the conversation tripped some lever in his mind. Reflex action sent him hurriedly to an inside pocket.

Making sure he's still got his wallet, thought Russell. This bit wasn't going to be easy. Sergeant would have handled the touch much better himself. That's if his conceit would have allowed it. Russell helped himself to a gherkin, a slice of ham.

" Now listen, Arthur. Paul needs two hundred and fifty quid. To-day. He's ready to cut you in on a full third of our next score. That's the long and short of it."

He caught Sam's eye. A girl bustled a cup of hot, strong tea to the table.

Little Arthur pulled himself a little nearer. He disliked people seeing his dangling feet. He had a grizzled moustache that he played with in moments of doubt.

" Two hundred and fifty quid ! That's a lot of money. No matter. Paul can beat a mug cleaner than the rest of them." He dropped his judicious attitude. " I'd be happier if he had a real live-wire to steer to him."

The Canadian showed good teeth in a smile without meaning. What could this chump know of the past four months—the ceaseless battle against Sergeant's indifference to work. Russell had no intention of losing his temper, however.

" Aren't you forgetting something, Arthur ? Paul taught me *how* to steer a mark. He's happy enough with the result."

Little Arthur switched to bonhomie, his tiny eyes crafty. " There you go, sport ! You've got as much sense of humour as a kangaroo. All I mean is that you've got to *produce*. You've got a mug lined-up—all right. Move him into any hotel you like. I'll fix up the money end with Paul."

Russell shoved the brew away. A lie—even half a lie— and this race-track Napoleon would do exactly what he was asked. But Sergeant preferred to sit back in saintly splendour while someone else cleaned stable for him.

"There *isn't* any mark," Russell said patiently. "Not yet, anyway. Paul wants the money to put up a front for his daughter. She's due in from California any moment."

Ryan blinked shocked surprise. "You're kidding! His daughter! Christ, Gordy, that's not a proposition!" He made an effort, his voice trailing off as if he disbelieved what he was saying. "I'd let him have maybe a few quid if it's of any help."

Russell was half-way out of his seat, leaving, when he looked in the mirror. A tall man was coming through the door from the street. The Canadian sat down again. Little Arthur's reaction was as fast as Russell's.

"You're on your own, Gordy—not with me."

There was just time for Russell to switch to an empty table. Detective-Sergeant Brace took the opposite chair. He was wearing the clothing almost standard with junior Flying Squad officers—charcoal-grey suit and black Homburg hat. His fine gaberdine trench coat struck a note of independence. Russell made neither move to escape nor to welcome.

Brace stretched out a long arm, capturing Russell's cigarette pack. He watched Little Arthur's hurried exit with satisfaction. The cop had a full mouth, brown curly hair and an easy manner. He nodded after the ex-jockey. Holding the pleasant smile, he pushed a folded newspaper across the table.

"Now I had an idea that Little Arthur would be your banker. Stick the fifty quid in here and leave it on the table."

Russell stared at the printed columns. He knew that he was shaking and was unable to do anything about it. His voice was toneless.

"You said to-night."

In spite of the noise, Brace made himself heard with discretion. "I changed my mind. I don't like people who can't keep a bargain. I'll take it now."

Over behind the bar, Rifkind was honing his blade, his eyes aloof. The sound in Russell's throat was desperate.

" Look, Brace—we've always come across before, haven't we ! You ought to know that we haven't made a nickel in four months. I can't imagine what you've been smoking—this crazy idea that it was us who beat this guy Baxter ! "

Brace retrieved his newspaper, folded it neatly and thrust it into his raincoat pocket. He leaned both elbows on the table.

" You're a bloody liar, Russell ! I've got some news for you. Baxter didn't sail on the *Queen*. He didn't like what you did to him and filed a complaint. He spent a long time describing the men who robbed him. One description's vague enough—but you he's got like a photograph ! "

Russell shrugged. It didn't matter that his general description might be that of half a dozen other con-men. Brace's mind was made up and the next move his.

The detective got to his feet. " Come on—there's a car outside." His grip on Russell's arm was light yet possessive. As they passed the bar, the Canadian tried to mouth a message. He had to send word to Sergeant. But Rifkind presented a broad back, his head deep in the cash register.

Outside in the squad car, the usual hard-nosed cop was at the wheel. Russell was placed in the back between Brace and the radio operator. Only a few heads turned as the car nosed its way along the narrow crowded street. Once into the broad sweep of Piccadilly, the long black vehicle was lost in the traffic. Off the Strand, they turned into a side street running up to Covent Garden. Shops and offices faced a dirty stone building. Open gates topped with spikes led to a yard. The driver of the police car pulled his vehicle in front of a side door. Russell followed Brace into the Charge Room.

Highly-polished linoleum divided the sensible strip of carpet. A counter ran at right angles to it, wall to wall. Beyond this a young constable stood at a desk writing.

Brace indicated a bench. He lifted a flap in the counter and went through. The letters C.I.D. were painted on the far door. Brace jerked his head in that direction.

" Is there anybody in there ? "

11

The constable was too inexperienced to hide his curiosity. "They're all in there, sir."

Brace answered the man's unspoken question. "Keep an eye on this joker for me." He disappeared into the detectives' room.

Russell sat on the bench. The front entrance of the station house was only a few yards away. Beyond the stone portico, a milkman was whistling his cart up the street. The constable left his desk, raised the counter flap and wedged himself into the open space. It was a position from which he could bar any dash for liberty with an outstretched leg. He offered Russell a pack of cigarettes without speaking.

That's how most of them were, thought the Canadian. The uniformed branch, at least. Dumb and decent. If he told this rookie that Brace was no more than a thief with a badge—a cop who's been in on fifty crooked deals—the chump wouldn't believe him. These guys did their job conscientiously and without malice. If they accepted the idea of a rogue cop it would never be of a man on their own strength.

Russell lit one of his own cigarettes. "Who's in charge here?"

The constable stretched, scratching comfortably where the sharp edge of wood caught beneath his shoulder blades. He seemed to have difficulty in framing his answer. "Inspector Weston—that's the uniform branch. What's the trouble?"

Russell made a pistol of thumb and forefinger, pointing it at the opening door. "Ask Brace—he's got all the answers."

The blue-clad inspector topped Brace by six inches. Rank insignia sparkled on sturdy shoulders. He had a long head thatched with hopeless hair and a soft West Country accent. "Is this the man?"

Brace leaned across the counter. "That's him, Inspector. And don't fall for that look of injured innocence. I'll tell you exactly what he's going to say—those bastards on the

12

Flying Squad never give him a break. In fact, there's no justice, is there, Gordy ? "

Russell ignored him, concentrating on Weston. The inspector wore old-fashioned boots. He covered his mouth with scrubbed square fingers, making no concession to the detective's sarcasm. " Do you know why you're here ? " Weston asked the Canadian.

Russell stood, carefully keeping his voice civil. Instinct told him he had to destroy the impression that Brace was creating. " Last night I came in here voluntarily to answer some questions that Sergeant Brace wanted to ask me. At one o'clock this morning they turned me loose. Now this. That's as much as I know."

Weston swivelled the Day Book round so that he could scan the pages. " There's no record here of this man being detained, Sergeant. Was any charge made against him ? "

Brace shook his head. " I was still making inquiries, sir."

Weston's expression was understanding. " Aye—and are you charging him now ? "

Brace's smile was both confident and fair. " I'd sooner answer that when the identification parade's over, sir."

Some of the strain went from Russell's legs. He'd been too long in the game not to know the legal significance of an identification parade. *To test fairly and adequately the witness's ability to recognise the accused person.* If this business was staged on the level, he had a chance. There was one card in his hand and it had to be played right. He addressed the inspector.

" Don't think I'm trying to be smart—but I want to know whether or not I'm in custody."

Weston's burr drove through Brace's raised voice. " The door's in front of you. As far as I'm concerned you can use it. What Detective-Sergeant Brace might do is another matter."

Russell blinked. If he walked out, Brace's next attack might come from any direction. Better an exposed threat than one hidden. If he could get by this parade, Brace wouldn't be likely to come at him again for a long while. Never for a moment did the Canadian take his eyes from Weston's face. He spoke quietly.

" No, I'll take a chance, Inspector. All I ask is that this thing's run straight."

Weston's mouth hardened. " I don't like this sort of talk in my station, Russell. Everyone gets a fair shake of the stick here, remember that ! Is two o'clock all right, Sergeant ? " He glanced at the wall clock.

Brace read his watch flamboyantly. " That barely gives me an hour, sir. I've got my witnesses to collect. Better make it three."

" We'll make it two," Weston said shortly. " You knew this case was coming up. Your witnesses ought to be on call."

There was a moment's silence broken by Brace. " I'll try to reach them by phone. Could I have a word with you in private, Inspector ? " The two men moved to the far end of the room. Brace gave his information in an undertone then left through the C.I.D. room.

From where Russell stood, the back end of the squad car showed as it turned from yard to street. Weston lifted the flap in the counter. " You'd better come through here. I don't want any of these witnesses getting a shot at you before the line-up." He led the way into the police canteen. A couple of constables were eating at a long table littered with dirty plates. Behind them a stout woman stood at a battery of pots. Weston lifted the lid on one of the pans, his nose lifting.

" This isn't the Savoy. But if you want a meal, it's here."

Russell took a chair at the table. From this seat, he controlled the yard through the window. The balance of feeling was delicate. The slightest hint of superiority was bound to offend Weston. He had to gamble on the inspector's integrity.

" I'll take whatever's going," said Russell quietly. He

faced dark meat and dank suet pudding with determination.

The two policemen finished their meal in a hurry and left. Weston's stride was taking him from one wall to the other. Suddenly he stopped.

" I suppose a fellow like you thinks he knows how an identification parade should be run ? " he challenged.

Russell kept his eyes on his plate. If he agreed, he'd be off to a wise guy's start—yet in the light of his police record, denial would sound like a direct lie. He emptied his mouth.

" I've been on two of them, Inspector. It happens that I don't think either was an indication of how they should be run."

Weston waved impatiently. " Don't think I'm going to ask you where ! Here, we do it according to the book. You can have your solicitor present or a friend. You know that, of course ? "

Russell nodded. A friend. Sergeant, for instance ! Sitting up in his apartment, chewing his knuckles and worrying about his daughter.

The Canadian lit a cigarette, thinking that it was time to start rationing them. It might well be a long night. " I don't want anybody here," he answered. " All I want is to get this thing over as quickly as possible. And I'm going to tell you this, Inspector, for what it's worth. I don't know the first thing about this charge."

" It isn't me you've got to convince," said Weston. " It's the witnesses." He went to the open window and called to the two men who had eaten in the canteen. Both had changed into civilian clothing. They came across the yard. Weston pointed at Russell. " I want you to go and pick up a dozen or so for an I.P. Get 'em as near his build and description as you can." One of the constables muttered something. " I *know* it isn't easy ! " said Weston quietly. " Tell them it's a civic duty. Tell them anything but get them ! "

The inspector turned away, his face morose. " You only see one side of it. Have you ever thought what it is,

inviting a man on the street to a police identification parade?
Either he's indignant that we think he looks like a thief or
scared of being picked out as one!" Ignoring the open
door to the yard, he started back towards the Charge
Room.

Russell hesitated before following. The woman at the
drying rack was putting on her coat. He spoke to her
quickly.

"Will you make a phone call for me when you go out?"
He put a lot into his expression. Respect, appeal, innocence.

She shook her head. "I ain't allowed to run messages.
Why don't you ask the inspector—he'd let you use the phone.
He barks but he don't bite." She took a last look at the
order of her utensils. "Good luck, dearie!"

He watched her square behind across the yard. He was
not sure what he might have told her to say to Sergeant.
This much was certain—if the parade went against him, he
had to get in touch with his partner. Sergeant would dig
up a lawyer from somewhere. There were still a few people
in town who'd chip in defence money—an instinctive act
of propitiation for continuance of their own liberty.

The yard gates outside had been closed. A group of men
was assembling under the direction of Weston and the
two constables. Some of them surveyed their surroundings
anxiously. One man stood apart, dark-suited and wearing
a bowler hat. His shoulders were squared. He gave the
impression that he was about to order a squad to come to
attention.

Inspector Weston lifted his head, shading his eyes against
the sun. "You've all volunteered to help on this identification parade. This is how it works. I'm going to ask you to
line up with another man. Two witnesses will try to pick
him out. Whether or not the man's guilty is no concern of
yours. I want you to keep facing your front—say nothing at
all unless you're told. Above all, pay no attention to the
man who's going to be there with you. Is that all clear?"

The man in the bowler hat had a voice that carried. "Not
bloody likely, it isn't! What happens if one of these

blighters picks *me* out ? Am I supposed to conduct my business from a cell ? "

A couple of the others changed legs, grinning nervously. Weston's frown killed any hint of levity. " I think I can guarantee your safety, sir. The man in custody is the only one who has anything to worry about." Russell moved away from the window as the inspector came up the steps to the canteen.

Weston nodded briskly. " Well, the witnesses are here. They'll be coming out into the yard one at a time. When the first one's finished, he'll be taken into my office through here. No chance to speak to the second witness on the way. Got it ? You can stand where you like and change your position on the line as often as you want."

The shake was back in Russell's hands. He followed the inspector stiff-legged to the yard. The men outside were standing in the shade. One of the constables was leaning against the closed gates. The other waited at the bottom of the canteen steps.

Russell cleared the huskiness from his throat, assuming an unfelt ease. " Where's Brace going to be while all this is going on ? "

For a moment it seemed as if Weston's patience were done. He stabbed a finger, viciously towards the main building. " Where he's *supposed* to be ! " he answered. He was close behind Russell as they walked into the sun-shine.

Russell took a quick look at the curious waiting faces. The military gentleman had appointed himself rank-marker. His bowler tipped over his nose, his stance was calculated to repel any assault on his person. Russell moved along the line, stopping in front of a man roughly his own weight and height. The stranger wore a hat and was dressed for an afternoon's horse racing. He edged off, allowing the Canadian to take place beside him. The yard was suddenly silent, the sound of outside traffic nearer than reality.

Weston was standing at the door to the Charge Room. He shouted his summons. As he did so, Russell slipped to the end of the line. The head in the bowler hat lifted next to him. He heard the man's short grunt. The first witness came into the bright glare, peering into the yard uncertainly. He was a short dark man with a heavy tan. Weston's outstretched arm stopped him.

" I want you to look at these men very carefully, Mr. Baxter. If you think you see the one who robbed you, just tap him on the shoulder." He made an entry in his notebook.

Baxter halted a dozen yards from the line. Eyes focused at head-level, he considered the group as a whole. Then very slowly he started his walk down the line.

High above a barred window, a pigeon was cleaning its feathers. Watching it, Russell lost all sense of time. It was a small bird, its plumage grimed with London dirt. It hopped peevishly, rejecting the sidling overtures of its mate.

The clicking of Baxter's gum drew nearer. He was breathing heavily, sometimes pausing a moment, passing his man cursorily at others. As the man drew near, Russell had the certainty that he would stop. Somehow, the Canadian managed to keep his eyes on the pigeons across the yard. Baxter stopped in front of the man with the bowler hat. He half-turned to the inspector, his voice uncertain.

" I can't see this guy's face—would you ask him to take off his hat ! "

The bowler hat was removed, exposing Baxter to its owner's glare. The witness was now definite. " No—I don't see the man I want here ! "

There was a general shuffling of feet as a constable herded Baxter up the canteen steps. Weston lifted his voice. " Send on the next witness ! " His back was to the windows of the Charge Room. For an instant, Brace's curly head showed there. It was the briefest movement—the innocent pass of a man crossing from one side of the room to the other.

But Russell saw it. Before the door opened on the second witness, he had moved again to the centre of the line. He stood next to the man in racing checks. Without a word, he lifted his neighbour's rakish trilby and put it on his own head.

Again Weston repeated his instructions, this time to a blue-haired woman in tussore suiting. She made it plain that she had no need of them. She conducted her inspection at a charge that carried her to the spot where Russell had been standing. She stared hard at the man facing her.

" I'm pretty sure this is the man, Officer. Of course it was night and he wasn't dressed this way . . . maybe if I could hear him speak ? "

Weston strode across the yard. " Is there anything in particular you want to hear him say, ma'am ? "

She spiked the ground with one heel, reflecting. " Ye-es. He had a funny way of saying ' Down under '."

The inspector's face was completely without humour. " Would you mind saying that, please—' Down under ' ? "

The man wet his shocked mouth and struggled the words out. The inspector waited, pencil on paper. " I'm afraid you'll have to make up your mind, ma'am. Is this the man or not ? "

It was the spur that the woman needed. Her tone took on fresh conviction. " It is. I'll swear to it ! That's him, all right ! "

The constable ushered her in to her waiting husband.

The line broke and the yard was alive with sudden chatter. The man next to Russell retrieved his hat with a grin. " It makes you think, old boy, doesn't it," he said thoughtfully. He started for the opening gates with a pleasant nod.

They were alone now—Russell, Weston and the two constables. The inspector snapped the elastic on his note-book and spoke to one of his men.

" Let me know as soon as the witnesses have gone. Are you satisfied ? " he turned to Russell. His own reaction was completely hidden. He was shading his eyes again, watching the door to the Charge Room. A constable waved a hand from the window.

Inside, Brace was waiting for them. He pushed aside a clump of springy hair, leaning on the counter easily. It was a sporting acceptance of defeat, perfectly done.

" Looks as though we'll have to let him go after all, Inspector."

Russell took a seat on the bench. He used four matches to light a cigarette and said nothing. Weston glanced at the wall clock and made an entry in the Day Book. His voice was noncommittal. " You're done with him ? "

Brace straightened up, his grin frank. " After that mess out there, what else ? But I'll tell you something, Inspector. I put those witnesses in a cab in front of the gates. From where we were, we could see you. *And* him. Both Mr. and Mrs. Baxter recognised him."

Weston moved the heavy ruler on top of the desk, his voice and expression unhelpful. " No doubt they did. But they did it a bit late, Sergeant. I'm going to let this man go unless you're preferring a charge."

Brace's shoulders dropped slightly. " Ah well—you don't get a coco-nut every time. But then neither do you, Gordy. Remember that." He lowered the flap in the counter carefully and was gone.

Weston and Russell were alone. The Canadian loosened his tie, keeping his place on the bench. Ash dropped at his feet. Using one hand, he fanned it under his seat. He looked up to find Weston watching him.

The inspector's voice was quiet. " What are you waiting for ? "

Russell slid an arm along the back rest. " You've been at it too long for me to tell you the score, Inspector. You heard Brace—you saw what went on outside. That identification parade was a put-up job. Neither of those witnesses had ever seen me before."

Weston held the ruler as if he would break it in half. " There's nothing else you want to say—no complaint? "

Russell considered. Expediency demanded the real issue between Brace and himself to be hidden. Yet the need to make his point was strong. Somewhere in Weston's hard head was an objective sense of fair play. Russell chose his words.

" I'm a thief, Inspector. I break the law—you administer it. We both run hazards. I want to ask you one question. What's your personal opinion of a crooked cop ? "

The policeman made no answer. Knowledge of freedom gave Russell's voice a bitter edge. Not for nothing did they portray Justice as a blindfolded woman with a pair of scales. Blindness was the key—the scales were make-weight.

" Go ahead and say it," he urged. " Any method's justifiable when you're dealing with people like me."

The ebony ruler was smashed down on the heavy book. Weston's face was a white fury. " I've *got* no words for people like you, Russell ! Aye—you can grin all you want. There must be people somewhere who gave you whatever decency's left in you. The next time you make a haul, think of *them* sitting there counting it with you. Now get out of here ! "

The echoing denunciation followed Russell into the bare lobby. In spite of himself, the Canadian took the steps to the street at the run. He walked south hurriedly, choosing the sunny side of the street. That old goat ! he mouthed. Full of righteousness and wrath as soon as he got near the truth. People like Little Arthur had the right angle—there ain't no such thing as a good cop, sport. I knew one once—finished up by nicking his grandmother.

Turning into the Strand, the Canadian headed for Trafalgar Square. It never varied, he remembered. The shortest trip to the cells left you with fresh appreciation of the ordinary. The passing girls—the horses in the brewer's dray—even the stink of burned gasoline. All had their place in a life suddenly worth living.

He turned into the big square, hesitant as he passed the telephone booths. Better maybe that he broke the news to Sergeant in person. The phone was still tapped. Something the inspector had said rankled. Russell was unable to resist self-justification. The rambling house in York Mills, three thousand miles away—the family in it—were all part of an unpleasant memory. As for decency, Weston should have been exposed to a household run for the benefit of one son only. And have been that son's younger brother.

He shut out the rest of the picture with determination and ran down the steps to the subway.

The quiet Knightsbridge square was still peaceful. A few more nursemaids pushed their charges the length of the shady gardens. The porter trundled Russell to the top floor. Sergeant opened immediately to the discreet tap. He had made some effort at cleaning the apartment. The table top was free of debris. Through the open bedroom door, the place was tidy.

The older man's voice was impatient. " For God's sake what's been going on ! I had Little Arthur on the line a couple of hours ago—sounding like a laying hen without a vent. What's this about you and Brace ? "

Russell's brusqueness was unaccustomed. Too much had happened over the past twenty-four hours. " Screw Little Arthur—you get *nothing* there ! Brace has had me into Bow St. again, Paul." He kept his account of the parade factual. Let Sergeant supply the colour later—he always did.

The other man's smooth cheeks bulged. He let the air out with a rush. " That does it, Gordy. I've got Lucy to think about. How can she come here with every knock on the door maybe a cop ! "

Russell stood at the window, watching the gardens. " So what are you going to do ? "

" I've been on to Pan American. They've got a plane out from New York to Paris that arrives at six to-morrow night. They'll try and get her on it—a cable will reach her at Idlewild. We'll meet her in Paris."

Sometimes, thought Russell, his partner was completely out of touch with reality. Usually when the situation involved that frisgig of a daughter of his. He tried to be patient.

" I'm not going to ask how we live there, Paul. Just how we get there. What we use for money."

Sergeant's voice was full of assurance. " I've got it

figured out, son. You find me a mark before midnight. We'll put him in at the Seat."

Russell's move from the window was fast. He had the catch down on the front door before Sergeant had shifted place. He spoke urgently. " The law's down below. Have you got anything here—any props ? " He went back to the curtain. " It's Brace. They'll be up in a couple of minutes, Paul ! " He felt perfectly relaxed—only the twitch in his lip had started up.

Sergeant nodded. " Take the latch off," he instructed. " I'm clean here—unless he's brought along something he intends to find ! "

They sat in the battered arm-chairs, waiting for the door buzzer to sound.

It was Russell who answered. Brace straddled the entrance, his outstretched arm supporting his weight. Another man stood behind him—young, with reddish hair and eyes that were set too close together.

Brace was civil. " You're going to let us in ? Remember the neighbours—we don't want a scene on the doorstep." The two detectives came into the living-room.

Sergeant had not moved from his chair. He sat with his back to the window, the top of his head silver in the sunshine. His plump face was composed.

Brace threw his hat at a chair. The sweep of his arm invited his companion to take in the scene. " See what I told you, Ned. They live more comfortably than we do —and manage to look twice as respectable."

The red-haired detective ran a finger along the door panel. He inspected the result with distaste. " But the place is filthy, Joe. Look at that dust ! Needs a woman's touch— wouldn't you say ? " He threw open doors to bedroom, bathroom and kitchen.

Brace went into the bedroom, came out carrying a small leather photo-frame. He pursed his mouth in a soft whistle and goggled at Sergeant.

" Where do you keep *her* ? " He handed the picture to his partner.

The man dropped the frame on the table. " Looks under age to me. It might be worth following up, Joe. Has he ever had a con for that sort of thing ? "

Russell came very close to him. " It's his daughter, Mac. One of these nights, we'll meet somewhere. And I'll stick that tongue of yours up your nose."

The old man's voice was sharp with authority. " Cut it out, Gordy ! " He looked up at Brace. " If this is a shake-down, Joe—you're out of order. I've always paid my way and you know it."

Brace shook his head in reproof. " What sort of talk's that to a police officer ! I've got information that there's stolen property on the premises—no search warrant—just a friendly visit. Have you got any objection if we look around ? "

Sergeant retrieved his daughter's picture. He touched Russell's arm. " Number seventy across the way—I want her to see this."

Neither detective made an attempt to stop Russell. He banged on the door on the other side of the corridor. The summons was answered as if the woman were waiting for it. She was dressed for the street—middle-aged with bright eyes under a short veil. She peered past Russell through the open door to Sergeant's flat. " Yes ? "

The Canadian stepped aside so that she had a better view. Ever since Sergeant had moved into the block, the woman's curiosity had been lively. Three or four times, she'd stopped Russell on the way up, with neighbourly advice. This he relayed, amused at his partner's horror.

Russell spoke without excitement. She must not be frightened, whatever happened. " Those two gentlemen are police officers, ma'am. There's no time to explain why but Mr. Sergeant has invited them to inspect his flat. He'd like you to be present."

She hesitated for a second. Using the hall mirror, she looked at herself narrowly, adjusting the veil at a more becoming angle. " Of course," she said quietly.

Russell led the way back to the living-room. Sergeant

whipped his chair under the woman with courtesy. She sat down, looking nervously from one man to the other.

The lines round Brace's mouth and eyes deepened. The nod at his partner left no confusion of identity. " We're police officers, miss. And this is police business."

With Sergeant and Russell at her side she seemed to gain confidence. " I know. This gentleman told me."

A little more than disgust showed in the red-headed detective's voice. There was caution. " Let's get out of here, Joe."

The Y-shaped vein in Brace's forehead distended. His usual smile was gone. " We'll do what we came here to do! " He stood in front of the woman speaking deliberately, " We're going to search this place for stolen property—with the owner's consent. If you want to watch, you're welcome."

The others were motionless as the detectives went about their business. Drawers were emptied, the contents spilled across the floor. The litter grew as the two men hauled and prodded. Dust flew as a curtain was jerked from its rail. Brace emptied the kitchen canisters, spewing salt, sugar and cereal into the sink. He was breathing heavily as he came back into the living-room. He poked a finger into a tear in the sofa cover, ripped the faded chintz to expose the original horse-hair. " All right, Ned ! " He straightened up, facing Sergeant. " I'd say you've got enemies, Sergeant. It looks as though this tip was a bad one. But if you want to make a complaint, you know where to do it." He turned to the woman. " I don't know if you've got anything worth stealing—if you have, I'd put it in the bank."

She stood as tall as she could make herself, hugging her bag to her stomach. " You're disgraceful—the pair of you ! I never saw anything like this in my life. I shall certainly report it to the proper authorities."

Brace stopped his partner in the hall and looked back. His poise was completely recovered. " You do whatever you want, miss. But you'd better make sure that you've got your facts straight. And I'd say you could do a lot better than getting them from a couple of con-men!" He closed the door gently behind him.

Russell waited at the curtain till the squad car was gone. It was four o'clock and already the day seemed too long. He turned to the woman, ready for any sign of disapproval. "Well, that's it. The show's over!"

She ignored him, her interest for the older man. "Mr. Sergeant! There must be some explanation for the way in which those men behaved!"

Sergeant was standing ankle-deep in papers that had been taken from the desk. Head slightly bent, he refused to meet her look. The attitude was familiar to Russell. Venerable and shamed I stand before you, he thought. And at that, it could be true. Sergeant's belief in his happier roles was implicit.

Russell took the woman by the elbow and guided her to the front door. "You've been more than kind, ma'am. It may interest you to know that you've prevented a miscarriage of justice." The phrase—the need to use it— irritated him. He still had his hand on the latch.

She backed reluctantly into the corridor. "I shall certainly make a report," she assured Russell. "I have a friend at the Home Office. But first I think I should know what it's all about."

He smiled, sure of her allegiance. "To-morrow," he promised and shut the door, waiting till he heard the tongue of her lock shoot home. Back in the living-room, Sergeant was kicking the litter under the table.

Russell spoke impulsively. "I'm sorry about all this, Paul. I should have known this was the sort of thing Brace would be likely to pull." He jerked his head at the front door. "If it hadn't been for her, we'd have been in trouble."

The older man's face was placid. "Maybe it's just as well. The rent's paid for a month—I can walk out any time I feel like it. I don't have to wait for the manager to give me the heave." He turned slowly, hunching his shoulders as he considered the wrecked apartment. "I'm sending

Lucy that cable—but not over *this* phone." He unscrewed the base of a plated candlestick and produced two five-pound notes. One he gave to Russell. " For expenses, Gordy. Stretch it—there's no more."

Russell tucked the bill in an inside pocket. " It's definite, is it ? You want me to find you a mark ? "

Sergeant's eyes were bright. " You've *got* to find me one ! I don't care where—that's your problem. I'm going to start packing—I'll be out of here in half an hour. I'm booking two seats on a plane to Paris for late to-night. I'll pay when I pick up the tickets. From five o'clock on, I'll be down at Rifkind's. Give me a ring there just as soon as you have any news."

Some of the older man's magic was back. A source of impulsion that banished Russell's doubt. He went into the bathroom and held his head under cold running water till pain invaded his temples. Finally he combed his hair carefully and used a dry towel to flick clean his shoes.

" I'll work the Knightsbridge area, Paul," he said. " Every hotel for a mile is lousy with visitors."

Sergeant's manner was diffident. " I don't have to tell you what this means to me, Gordy ? "

Russell shook his head. " You don't, Pop. You go ahead and do what you said. Above all, don't move from Rifkind's phone." He nodded good-bye. Whatever this was—this strength that came from being needed—was incapable of being expressed in words.

He shut the door to Sergeant's apartment and stood stock-still in the corridor. Five seconds elapsed then the woman's face peered round her own door. He came a step nearer, dropping his voice in a whisper.

" Mr. Sergeant's compliments—he's leaving for Scotland immediately. Explanations will have to wait till his return."

She breathed her reply as if caught in some conspiracy. " All right—tell him ' good luck ' ! "

CHAPTER II

TUESDAY P.M.

IT WAS half-past four when Stan Slezak pushed open the door of the Regent St. office. The far end of the room was covered with an enormous map of the world. The lighted red lines that traversed it were graphic indication of the airline's far-flung facilities. The girl who sat behind the desk had the impersonal brightness of the trained receptionist.

" May I help you, sir ? "

Slezak touched the visor of his cap in salute. " Captain Slezak—I have an appointment with the District Personnel Manager." He gave her the benefit of his biggest smile. A company rule prohibited fraternisation between air and ground staff. It wouldn't apply to him much longer. He collapsed in one of the deep leather chairs, stretching his long legs to the fullest extent. The prospect of the coming interview no longer disturbed him. Now that it was imminent, he was even relaxed. The organisation could only stage his dismissal in one way. They wanted neither undesirable publicity nor trouble with the Pilots' Union. Whistling through his teeth, he watched the girl at the intercom. Unlikely that she'd know anything—they'd need as much secrecy as they could get.

The girl touched a switch on the box in front of her. The vacation tan on her neck and arms had been carefully preserved. She touched the back of her neck self-consciously under his stare.

" Mr. Loefler will see you now, Captain. It's the third door along on your left."

Slezak saluted flamboyantly, half-closing an eye. The thin stuff of his uniform strained across his broad back. " Keep a little for me, honey ! " he kidded and left the room, pleased with himself.

Two men were waiting for him. One sat at a desk underneath the window. The other was in a chair off to the right. Removing his cap, Slezak took the only vacant seat.

Loefler flipped a hand at the third man. " This is Mr. Abel—company security officer."

Abel's head sat low on his shoulders. He nursed a large manila folder on his knees. He said nothing and made no acknowledgment.

Loefler was curt. " I don't propose to waste anybody's time, Slezak. And I'm not going to talk ethics to you. We're satisfied to break a smuggling ring before it gets under way." He tapped the papers in front of him. " I have a prepared statement here—it deals with your part in these activities as best we know it. Either you sign it together with your resignation or face a prosecution." His bald head lifted.

Folding both arms, Slezak leaned back easily. " I was going to say—keep your ethics for the board room ! I'll still make the point ! I'm forty years of age. In five years, you'd have grounded me. Or maybe I'd have been retired on a pension that wouldn't keep me in shoe leather."

Still relaxed, he came forward with a quick easy movement to take Loefler's wrist in the vice of strong fingers. Deep in the half-opened door on the other side of the desk, the tape decks turned on a small recording machine. He lifted a spool, sending the wire spiralling to the floor.

" We'll keep this *off* the record ! Here's a nice simple equation, Loefler. One that every business man should understand. In New York, gold's worth X. In the Far East it's worth X plus. ' Freedom from want ' " he quoted. " That's what I was doing, protecting my priceless heritage." He took a pen from the desk top, bending his crew-cut head. " I'll sign this bit of light literature—meanwhile, you can have the accountant make up my salary. Severance pay and two thousand dollars in paid-up superannuation. I'll take it in cash and U.S. currency. No cheques."

Loefler lifted the manila envelope. " We've been taking

a harder look at your war record, Slezak. Even then you had your own ideas about right and wrong, didn't you ? "

Slezak's mouth was wide as he stood over the security officer. The pilot took the envelope and ripped it across the middle. He tossed the fragments back in Abel's lap. " For an old man you talk too much. I ought to break your jaw ! "

Loefler's face was grey and strained. He had trouble in speaking.

" I'm making it a personal issue to see you never fly again, Slezak. I'll have you blacklisted from here to Tokyo."

The pilot balled heavy shoulders. " You're breaking my heart. Look—get the money. I want out of here ! "

Loefler spoke curtly into the intercom. " There's an envelope with Mr. Farrell. Have it brought to my office immediately."

He counted out thirty-four hundred dollars, fanning the bills across the desk. Slezak tucked the money in his breast pocket. He signed the discharge slip with a flourish. At the door, he turned and saluted again.

" If you're ever up a creek try the Ritz—that's where you'll find me ! "

He flagged a cab on Piccadilly Circus. " Grey's Hotel. That's the corner of Sloane Street and Knightsbridge."

His room was at the back, one of three that the company held permanently for its pilots. Stripping to his shorts, he stretched out on the bed. Beirut and that phone call were no more than three days away. A whispering voice in chichi English had told him that the gold runs were over. Just that. Whatever Fassi might have known about an investigation he kept to himself. No warning—no thanks— no bonus. The Syrian had gone as he'd come—a mysterious sound at the end of a scratchy telephone wire.

Slezak drew his knees up—the bedcover smooth under his back. For the last six months, the living had been easy. In New York, he'd stood in shirt-sleeves in the back room of a West Side delicatessen while a webbed silk harness was strapped on him. The weight round his middle grew as the pock-marked old man dropped each ingot into its slot. He'd slept in this very hotel room, a small fortune in gold under his mattress. The end of the line was a tea-merchant's house in Bombay. A cool white building where the breeze from an overhead fan fluttered the hundred dollar bills on the bamboo table. A thousand bucks a run, it had paid. And it looked like going on for ever. Whatever he'd earned with Fassi he'd spent. Now he was through. But not the Syrian. Somewhere—somebody else would be strapping on the harness. People like Fassi had the right idea—the essence of crime was in its discovery, not in its nature. The rest was for the birds.

He lay for twenty minutes in a tub of hot water. Relaxed, he started to dress. At times, the interview with Loefler had seemed like a barred door at the end of a passage. The future beyond it unknown and perilous. Now that he'd passed it, he liked what he saw.

He brushed his hair vigorously. The civilian clothes he had with him were newly pressed. He settled the hang of the tropical suiting. The money Loefler had given him was still on the bed. He took out two thousand dollars. They made a comforting bulge at the back of his wallet. The rest he placed in an envelope. Sealing it, he wrote his name and room number on the front. The kind of people he was looking for would have no time for deadbeats.

Downstairs, he found a desk-clerk he knew. He gave him the sealed package of money. " Put this away for me, Frank. I'll get it in the morning."

The clerk nodded. " In the safe, Captain. Will you be leaving us again to-morrow ? "

Slezak hesitated. Normally he would have flown the westbound flight to Idlewild. He'd stick the company for this room as long as he could. Something in the man's face prompted him. " I dunno yet, Frank. I haven't been briefed. What makes you ask ? "

The clerk shrugged. " Only that Mr. Loefler phoned. He said you'd be checking out in the morning."

Slezak nodded. " Then there's probably a message for me in the Crew Room. I'll let you know ! "

It was seven o'clock. The hotel lobby was filling. A few mink capes and dinner jackets—two small scrubbed boys self-conscious in long trousers. The chink of silver in the restaurant reminded him of food. It was still early. Everything was right to-night—the feel of clean linen—no ban on drinking twenty-four hours before take-off—the money in his pocket. He'd have a drink here—drift east later.

The bar was crowded. He found a slot near the door that led to the side street. He ordered, watching with interest as the barman thumbed the cork from a half-bottle of champagne. Taking his glass, Slezak stepped back, feeling the tang on the back of his teeth. He lurched as an arm touched his shoulder. The wine slopped from his glass, spattering the shoes of the man who pushed to the bar.

The newcomer's tanned face showed concern. " That's the hell of a thing to do—I'm sorry." He wore soft grey tweeds and had a North American accent. He kicked the drops from the tip of a black brogue. " Here—let me get you a refill ! "

Slezak stepped back, making room at the bar. " Forget it ! " He held his glass out to the barman.

The stranger shrugged, giving his own order. He half-turned to Slezak, his smile rueful. " A little too anxious, I guess. I wanted to wash the dust out of my mouth. I've been on my feet since nine o'clock this morning."

Slezak hoisted his weight on a stool. The man's clothes could have come from any good tailor. But the voice was a give-away. " You're an American ? " asked Slezak.

" Canadian. From Toronto. I'd say you were a long way from home, too." The man took the next stool, pulling it round so that they faced one another.

Slezak emptied his glass. There was wine left in the bottle. He nodded at the barman. Lying on the bed upstairs, his scheme had seemed workable. All it needed was careful production. The Canadian was a perfect audience for a dress rehearsal.

Slezak put the right weight of meaning into his voice. "In my job, you're *always* a long way from home." He dropped heavy lids, masking his thorough inspection of the silk shirt, the square well-kept hands. Above all, the expression in the Canadian's eyes. This guy was incapable of hiding his need of a friendly ear. Slezak looked up, tapping the guide-book in front of the other. "I take it this is your first trip to London. You're doing it the hard way!"

The Canadian shrugged. "Could be! Back home it all sounded much easier. Toronto, I said—but I work up in Cobalt, Ontario. I'm a mining engineer. When you live like this for nine months in the year, *anything* is welcome, even a conducted tour!" He pulled a couple of snapshots from his pocket.

Slezak studied the prints. Fur-capped, wearing breeches, boots and a lumber jacket, the Canadian was standing against a mine-shaft. The background was bleak and snow-bound. Another drink, thought Slezak, and the guy'd have them both on some frozen rock-pile. He handed back the snapshots, taking a hold on the conversation.

"That's a little different to the territory I cover." He described the run from Lebanon to Bombay, touching on the dirt, heat and mystery of a half-dozen cities. Then he waited for the question he knew must come.

The Canadian was sipping his Scotch and water slowly—holding the glass as if it were to be his last. "What's that mean—oil?"

Slezak shook his head. He opened his hand, exposing the celluloid-covered card. The identification that took him into any of the airlines' installations. The image in his mind grew sharper. Later he would know when to use it. For now, the test was to keep this guy's interest hooked. He nodded at a table against the wall. "I'm a security officer. Why don't we take our drinks over there—it's quieter."

The Canadian followed, his face puzzled. " I wouldn't know how an airline uses security. Sabotage ? " he hazarded.

Slezak's smile was very broad. " Well, we do have guys who cover that field—my job's a little more specialised." The wine was hitting his nerve centres. He leaned across the table, playing the part of a man who talked a little too much. His voice was soft. " One dishonest pilot can touch off a great deal of trouble for the State Department— let alone an airline. Nobody likes gold smuggled across the border."

The Canadian's face was incredulous. " A pilot ? You're kidding, surely ! " He shifted uncomfortably as though the idea bothered him. " You don't find a crook at a control wheel any more than in a . . ." He tried to complete the image and failed. " You're kidding ! " he repeated.

Slezak ordered a couple of drinks. The line from ear to chin was hard. Nevertheless he had a job keeping his mouth straight. He waited till the barman had gone. " Am I ? What do you think these guys are—Boy Scouts ? Slezak's my name ! "

The Canadian's hand came up in acknowledgment. " Miller—Bob Miller ! "

Slezak leaned back with eyes half-closed. " You live in a different world, Miller. In the Far East they've another approach to this sort of thing. And the East is where these pilots take a fall. Those chichi bastards will proposition anybody ! " He spiralled smoke lazily, letting the accent on the last word linger.

The Canadian was frankly curious. " Maybe I shouldn't ask this, but what's London got to do with the Far East ? "

" Everything," answered Slezak. " This racket starts in New York and finishes in Bombay but the pay-off is right here." He laid his wallet on the table so that the edge of his big bills peeped out. He covered them quickly with his hand. " There's enough there to buy a slug of gold that will fit in a pilot's hip-pocket. In Bombay that slug's worth three times as much. It'll give you some idea of the incentive." He yawned openly, suddenly indifferent to the other's reaction. There was still a lot of work to be done on this story. Right now, it creaked. But he'd tell it again and again till he hit the right joker. And when he did . . .

He stood up. "It's been a pleasure, Miller. See you around."

The Canadian shook his head. "I'll be honest with you—I never got as close to a thing like this before. Let me buy you one for the road!"

Slezak hesitated. As far as he was concerned, the production was over. But if this guy still wanted to applaud well enough. He dropped back in the chair. "The last— I've got to eat!" He pointed in answer to the other's inquiry. "The can? Through the hotel lobby and on your right. There's a sign on the door!"

It was five minutes before the Canadian was back. The long room had emptied. Behind his counter, the barman was studying the racing results. For the next quarter-hour, Slezak added colour to his portrayal of a security officer with few illusions. Each point was made obliquely and with a total lack of moral judgment. He told of the fortune the smuggling ring was making—the irony of having been approached by them himself.

The Canadian listened in silence, his chin propped in a hand, eyes vaguely on the revolving door to the street. He pushed the ash-tray away from him, his expression obscure.

"You make it sound as though there's no real harm in what these guys are doing. O.K. Maybe twenty years ago this *wouldn't* have been a crime. But right now these men are breaking the law. It seems to me that would be enough for most people."

Slezak moved an impatient shoulder. "Ah, come off it! The only thing that keeps our hands out of each other's pockets in this day and age is fear. Fear of the consequences. That's good for everyone. You—me—even Deacon Joe over there!" He nodded at the small stout man passing through the bar.

As the glass door to the street rotated, the stranger dropped something that fell to the carpet. Slezak crossed the room and picked up a worn wallet. By the time he reached the street, its owner was lost in the crowd. Slezak went back to his table. The Canadian had not moved. Slezak put the wallet down between them. The uncertainty in the other man's eyes amused him.

"O.K.—let's speculate! An exercise in honesty. You saw the guy drop this wallet. Your theory is that if I hand it across the bar, the owner'll get it back. Right?"

The Canadian frowned, moving uncomfortably on his chair. "Hold on! My theory is that most people are honest by training if not by instinct. Whether or not the guy would get his wallet back—God alone knows. It could be the first time the man was ever in the place!"

Slezak's smile was openly superior. "Exactly. And because of that, this wallet wouldn't move any farther than the bartender's pocket. So we do this!" He tipped out the contents of the wallet. First was a Social Security card in the name of John Clancy. Then a copy of a will and a newspaper clipping. Four pound notes and some religious medals wrapped in a piece of silk.

Slezak was watching the Canadian closely. He knew that the man was having a hard time curbing his curiosity. Slezak shook open the newspaper cutting. A hotel bill fell out. Ignoring this, Slezak concentrated on the cutting. It had been clipped from the Stop Press column of a London paper. The date at the top was a month old.

WINDFALL FOR NEW YORKER

New York State courts have awarded property worth £150,000 to Mr. John Clancy of Queen's Borough, Brooklyn. Rival claimant to the estate was Miss Zoe Han, a nurse who had cared for the deceased property-owner. The judge dismissed Miss Han's claim as frivolous and completely without legal validity. Mr. Clancy, said the judge, was the sole surviving relative and must succeed in his action.

Two codicils to the will at issue were equally binding on the estate. These were as follows. The heir is bound to give the sum of ten thousand pounds to a charitable cause designated by the Pope. The heir must further distribute thirty thousand pounds to persons who live or work among the poor. This gift must be made in person by the heir, irrespective of race, creed or nationality.

Slezak looked at the copy of the will. The name of a prominent Wall Street lawyer was stamped across it. He tossed the clipping across the table.

The Canadian read the report very carefully then whistled softly. " This stuff must be important to the guy—he'll be climbing the wall."

Slezak controlled his excitement. At the back of his mind was the growing assurance that his evening had not been wasted. " Read it again," he said. " With nearly a quarter-million dollars, nobody worries ! "

The Canadian took the hotel bill from the papers in front of him and went to the bar phone. After a while, he looked across at Slezak, covering the mouthpiece with one hand. " He's back at his hotel. Wants us to take the wallet there."

" Tell him ten minutes." Slezak stood up. Putting back the papers, he pocketed the wallet.

It was an address north of the park. At Marble Arch, the driver swung left and stopped. The hotel sprawled the length of the entire block. They climbed the steps and into the brightly lit lobby, Slezak in the lead.

" What's his room number ? " The pilot's eyes followed the Canadian's pointing hand. Clancy was standing twenty yards away, facing the hotel entrance. He looked lost and his plump face was concerned.

They made their way across to him. Slezak pushed out a hand. " Mr. Clancy ? I'm Stan Slezak. I have your wallet." Smiling, he handed over the worn leather folder.

Clancy riffed through the contents, fastening on the religious medals with evident relief. His accent was

Brooklyn with a hint of brogue. " You're very kind. Most of this junk doesn't matter but the medals belonged to my wife. I've got you both to thank. It does my heart good that you're Americans." A head shorter than either, he took each man by the elbow and steered them towards a smoking-room. Here he sat between them, beaming, till a waiter answered his signal. His voice was insistent.

" I want you men to have the best in the house. Unfortunately I need to take a little hot peppermint myself. After every meal. Doctor Kelly's a hard man." He touched his stout stomach.

" Make mine coffee," answered Slezak. " I haven't eaten yet."

Clancy's manner was excited. " But I want to show my appreciation. There's no limit to what I'd have paid to get Bridie's medals back, God rest her soul ! And I'm a rich man." He drew out the newspaper clipping and leant back sipping his hot coloured water.

" We read it," said Slezak shortly. " Before we found your address."

The Irish-American's face was proud. His brogue grew thicker with excitement. " There's few that hasn't heard of John Clancy. Since I got my money, there isn't a charitable organisation that hasn't been after it. And three months ago, not the time of the day could I get from anyone. I want Uncle Matt's money to go where it'll do some good." Calling the waiter, he paid the bill with a pound from the shabby wallet. He hitched his chair closer, dropping his voice. " It's a big responsibility for a simple man. Just looking at the pair of you, I had an idea. Sez I, Bridie would have set her heart on it. You'll sit here, both of you, while I go to the cashier feller."

They watched him through the swing doors and across the lobby. A dumpy figure, slightly forlorn in front of the ornate cashier's desk.

The Canadian's voice was suddenly husky. " They say charity starts at home, don't they ? Last winter it hit twenty degrees below up in Cobalt. I saw whole families of kids forced to stay away from school for months on end. Not enough of anything. Grub, clothes or fuel ! ''

Slezak's eyes were still on Clancy. The door to the cashier's safe was wide open. This Canadian had to be got rid of as soon as possible, thought Slezak. Permanently and without creating any suspicion. Clancy's jackpot was going one way—not two. As the old man started back towards them, Slezak spoke in a hurry.

" You let him make his own decisions. You heard what he said—he thinks every man and his uncle's after his dough ! ''

Clancy sat down clutching a red-sealed package. The bank stamp across the heavy paper was just decipherable. " Now," he said. " I've got a proposition for you men. You can say ' yes ' or you can say ' no '—but you'll still eat the best meal this place can cook—on me." He studied the expression on their faces. First Slezak's then the Canadian's. His voice was soft. " I know honest faces when I see them. I'm an old man. And old men get set in their ways. Will ye ever tell me this—how about helping me distribute some of Uncle Matt's money ? '' For the moment both men were silent. Clancy went on. " The lawyers give me a free hand. I'd meet your expenses and there'd be something else at the end to show for your trouble.''

Before Slezak was able to stop him, the Canadian had answered. " I work for a mining concern, Mr. Clancy. For people like me salaries are high. It's a different story for unskilled labour. They come up from Southern Ontario in their thousands. The first big freeze and they're laid off without a hope of getting through the winter. I live among these people. They need help. I'd be glad to do what I can without expenses or reward.''

Clancy's eyes showed approval. " It does you credit, son. How about you, sir ? ''

Slezak took time to answer. More than ever he was regretting the Canadian. The guy was a headache—all this nobility. Slezak leaned his weight on his elbows, his gaze direct and frank. If this old bum wanted self-sacrifice, he'd get it.

" I'm a law enforcement officer, Mr. Clancy. What free time I get back at home I give to an organisation for the reform of criminals. I'm a single man and it gives me pleasure. Once in fifty times, we manage to get an ex-con straightened out. That makes it worth while. And we always need money."

Clancy's head had been bent in attention. He looked up. " There's good in everyone—it's just got to be found. A better man than me said that. Uncle Matt's character's written in every line of the will he made. It's time I did more than talk. We've got to have faith in one another if we're going to work together." His fingers trembled slightly on the package but his look for the Canadian was without fear. " There's twenty thousand dollars here, son. I want you to take charge of it—go with your friend for a walk round the block. I'll be sitting right here when you come back."

The Canadian stood up. He pushed the package of money into the top of his trousers. The tension of his belt kept it in position. He buttoned his jacket. Slezak went after him in a hurry. They stood for a moment on the steps outside the hotel entrance.

Slezak considered the slant of the other's sunburned jaw with narrow eyes. One good hook would put the guy on the deck but then what—a free-for-all with a hundred window-shoppers as an audience. The cops in the doorway opposite. No—another formula was needed.

" Well—let's go," he said suddenly. " We'll walk the block, the way he said."

The Canadian seemed edgy, veering from each passer-by, one hand protecting the money under his belt. On their return, he stopped at the top of the hotel steps and spoke to Slezak. " This guy's crazy or completely innocent. Either way, they'll have the shirt off his back if we don't give him a hand."

Clancy was where they had left him. He put down his

newspaper, his face peaceful. Taking off old-fashioned spectacles, he wiped the corners of his eyes.

The Canadian handed back the sealed package. " Put that away where it belongs," he advised. He pulled his own wallet from his pocket and gave it to Clancy. He grinned. " *You* sweat this time. Most of it's in traveller's cheques but they're good Canadian dollars."

Slezak walked to the street, easing his stride to Clancy's short steps. They had covered half the block before the old man spoke.

" Your friend's the stamp of the son Bridie and I might have had if the good Lord had blessed us."

Slezak was cautious. One wrong word and this fat hairbag would be off—holding the Canadian by the hand. He made himself heavily enthusiastic. " They don't come any better."

He recrossed the lobby. The time had come for him to make the same ridiculous gesture as the others. This Canadian was obviously in as far as Clancy was concerned.

Slezak pushed his wallet at the younger man. " Every nickel's counted. Don't forget you've got two months' salary there."

The Canadian smiled good-humouredly. He peeped at the thick sheaf of bills in Slezak's wallet. " You guys live too well." His step was unhurried as he followed Clancy from the smoke-room.

It was fifteen minutes before Slezak moved. When he did, it was at the run. Outside on the street, he made a dash to circle the block, scattering pedestrians as he went. By the time he was back in the hotel, and at the receptionist's desk, he was out of breath.

The clerk spun the circular file. " Mr. John Clancy ? I'm afraid we have nobody of that name registered, sir ! "

CHAPTER III

TUESDAY P.M.

CLOSING THE GLASS partition, Russell sat with his back to the cab-driver. He searched Slezak's wallet thoroughly, tossing the sheaf of bills into Sergeant's lap.

"I've kept three hundred bucks. You can owe me the rest of my end—you're going to need it."

Sergeant sat straight. The brogue was now quite gone from his voice. "You're a good friend, Gordy. Here's what you do. Let me off somewhere near the B.E.A. offices. I'll pick up our bags and take a car out to the airport. Your ticket I'll leave at the inquiry desk in the main building. Pay this cab off at Victoria Station—and see that mug gets the rest of his junk back. Don't forget—we don't know one another till we're airborne." He held on firmly as the cab swung out to overtake.

Red lights at the bottom of Park Lane halted the cab. Russell slid the glass panel back. "Stop at Piccadilly Circus. My friend gets out there."

The driver turned east. The sidewalk traffic had the aimless flow of a hot summer's night. The women in sleeveless dresses—many of the men carrying their jackets over their arms. As the cab passed Down Street, Russell ducked, fumbling at a shoe. A squad car was parked on the intersection, its front ready to be turned east or west into Piccadilly.

Leaning over, Sergeant gripped Russell below the knee. "Take it easy—those chumps don't know we're alive."

Russell shifted uncomfortably. The pattern hadn't changed through the years. Always he could plan and execute with certainty. Yet success left him convinced that his guilt was communicable. It could be a face in a crowd

—the sudden memory of a clue he might have left—even the physical possession of stolen money—any of these was capable of unnerving him. It was a torment that vanished after a day's continued freedom. But during that time, he had to have his partner's reassurance. With Sergeant there was no need to hide his weakness.

"I don't like it, Paul," he said nervously. "That pilot's going to be hostile—if ever Brace gets hold of him it'll mean real trouble." He waited for Sergeant's denial.

The old man blew disdain with his cigar smoke. "I've handled too many marks with larceny in their hearts. That guy's a born thief. It's just as well you gave me his name when you called Rifkind's. I phoned his company—nobody wanted to talk about Mr. Slezak. In fact he doesn't work there any longer."

Russell licked dry lips. "See what I mean—a smart bastard. Another thing—that cashier at the hotel. For God's sake, Paul! You want to make certain he recognises you? All that backing and filling with the package in and out the safe. . . ."

The lights at Piccadilly Circus were nearing. Sergeant donned heavy-rimmed spectacles and a hat. His voice was just short of smug. "He never *saw* any package! I made it up at the apartment and had it under my jacket. All I asked him was the day's dollar rate against pounds. What's to remember?" His hand was on the door handle. "You get yourself a drink and relax, Gordy. Do you think you'll be all right, son?" Real concern was in his face as he inspected Russell closely.

The Canadian turned his wrists, considering fingers that were without any tremor. If Sergeant were right, maybe Slezak wouldn't go near the cops. In which case, his fears were gratuitous wear and tear on an overworked nervous system. He answered irritably.

"Of course I'll be all right. I'll see you at the airport."

He paid off the cab at Victoria Station. Buying a single ticket to Brighton, he held up the queue with idiotic inquiry.

If ever this clerk were asked, Russell wanted to be remembered. By now, he employed Sergeant's rearguard manoeuvres without doubt of their reason.

He walked through the station and into the hotel. At the desk he asked for an envelope large enough to take Slezak's wallet. Showing his face at this stage was without meaning. Scribbling Slezak's name and hotel on the package, he dropped the envelope into the mail chute. It was gone nine and the plane took off at midnight. He lost himself in the crowd in the station buffet. A brandy and soda washed down dehydrated sandwiches. For a while he sat surrounded by harassed parents in constant search of baggage or children.

If everything were as simple as Sergeant claimed, he thought, why hadn't they ridden out to the airport together ! The old man had been acting and thinking irrationally ever since that goddam cable arrived. Nothing seemed to matter to him except his daughter. Russell remembered the frustrations of the past months with irritation. Every suggestion he had made over this period had been hit with criticism from his partner. His views were either dangerous or impractical. Yet one bleat from Lucy and Sergeant had them both taking chances no grafter in his right mind would have considered.

If they ever *got* to Paris, it would be even worse. What made a girl travel six thousand miles to see a father she didn't even know—what else but money ! She'd lower the boom on the old man and there'd be no peace till she got what she wanted.

He got up to thread his way through a trio of bawling children. Far better to be on the move than sit here dreaming up fresh trouble. The next hour or two were likely to hold enough.

He rode the subway to the end of the line. At Uxbridge, he boarded a bus that deposited him at the main airport building. He hurried in and used the escalator up to the vast hall, still busy in spite of the late hour. To his left and right were the numbered traffic channels. Stores, a news-stand and telephone booths flanked a further flight of stairs. He walked over to the inquiry desk.

Two feet away, the girl's lips moved almost soundlessly, her voice reverberating from the P.A. speakers. He tried to bring some ease to his manner.

" I believe you've got an airplane ticket here for me—the name is Gordon Russell."

The girl skimmed a pile of papers and vouchers. She looked up, checking with the outsize clock on the wall above her. "Yes, Mr. Russell. B.E.A. flight 707. It'll be Channel Two at twenty-three hours forty."

Only a few people sat at the bar. A long-haired blonde wearing dark glasses, a middle-aged Hindu couple, festooned with cameras and Sergeant. The old man sat at the end of the row, champing a bun, his attention apparently for his newspaper. He looked up at Russell's reflection in the bar mirror. His eyes were without recognition.

Russell walked on down the hall. There was nowhere he would be out of the way. He needed a drink again. But as long as Sergeant sat where he was, this was impossible. They must avoid one another till they were safely aboard the plane. As Russell made his turn at the far end of the hall, he saw his partner walking slowly towards Channel Two.

Hurrying to the bar, Russell gulped a stiff shot of brandy. Lifting the glass, he saw the face behind him in the mirror. A young man, leaning against the pillar. Hatless and wearing a club tie and flannel suit. The impression the man made was a little too innocent. Scotland Yard had twenty like this joker. Young, keen and with what passed for the Oxford accent taking the edge from their professional zeal.

Russell slid a couple of coins across the counter and walked up the stairs to a telephone booth. Lifting the receiver, he pantomimed a call. It was hot in the confined space and he was sweating. He looked down to the hall below. The man in the flannel suit was coming up the stairs.

Russell talked into a dead mouthpiece. Fifty yards away, Sergeant was sitting comfortably in an arm-chair, chatting with the blue-clad hostess. The stranger had paid no attention at all to the old man. A cop's nose must have led him up the stairs, thought Russell. Or a face remembered from the Rogue's Gallery. Russell's back itched as the man took up position outside the booth. It seemed he was content to wait.

The P.A. system boomed suddenly, its message invading the booth. "B.E.A. passengers travelling to Paris by Flight 707 are requested to proceed to Channel Two immediately for customs and immigration inspection." The girl repeated her instructions in French.

Sergeant had gathered his brief-case. He was looking back towards the bar. Russell buttoned his jacket and opened the door of the booth. The man's voice was as he'd expected. Civil and direct.

"You wouldn't happen to have change for sixpence? I've got to make a phone call."

Pushing four pennies into the man's hand without a word, Russell ran down the stairs. He was the last passenger into the channel. As the hostess gave him his boarding card, he looked up at the phone booths. There was no sign of the man in the flannel suit.

Russell took his place in the line. He moved into the customs hall a dozen yards behind Sergeant. Passengers at the far end were producing their passports for immigration control. Two Special Branch men in plain clothes stood behind a desk.

The routine was all too familiar. The first official took the passport, flipping it open at the photograph. A quick comparison with the original and the passport was handed to his companion in the chair. The next ten seconds were the worst. You had to stand there—your passport out of sight beneath the overhang of the desk. If you were a wanted man, it could be your name, description, even your accent that might betray you. If you were wanted badly enough, false identification was no guarantee of safety. The rule was never to use a phony passport in the country of its origin. On that score he was safe enough. The Canadian passport in his hand was genuine. In Paris, if he needed it, a hundred and fifty dollars would buy a satisfactory alternative.

He shuffled forward. Sergeant was already beyond the check-point. You had to know the old man to recognise the relief in the set of his head and shoulders.

" Mr. Russell ? " The official ran his pencil down the passenger list, ticking off the name. He looked up. Hard, strained eyes seemed to commit the Canadian to memory and then dismiss him.

Russell pocketed his passport and walked on, willing himself not to turn round. There had been no sign of his bags but Paul must have collected them. By now, the manageress of his small hotel was unmoved by his comings and goings. Six months' rent in advance kept Mrs. Jenner tolerant of her star boarder. The locked, battered wardrobe trunk would have defeated Sergeant. It didn't matter—all that it held could be duplicated in Paris. Doc Springer always had a supply of share certificates for sale. Authentic note-paper filched from the offices of half a dozen banks, fake credit cards. All the tools they would need now that they were back in action.

He followed the group to the tarmac. A couple of hundred yards away, jet engines screamed in the warm darkness. The sound gave him confidence. He turned his head for the first time. Beyond the windows of the lighted building the Special Branch officers were starting up cigarettes, indifferent to the passengers boarding the plane.

Hurrying, Russell took the vacant seat beside his partner. There was a surge of power before the night rushed at them. Then a feeling of suspension—almost without sense of motion. He unbuckled his seat belt, stretching his legs as far as they would go.

Sergeant snapped on the light above his head. " You cut that pretty fine, Gordy ! For a moment I thought you'd missed the plane. What happened—did you think you saw someone ? " The eyes were shrewd yet kind.

Russell nodded down the aisle where the Hindu woman

47

was settling her sari. " More or less—I had her pegged as Brace in a skirt." He wanted to forget the agony of the telephone booth.

Sergeant crossed his hands on his stomach and closed his eyes. His voice was pitched not to carry to the seat in front. " I was watching you. When that cop put his cross or whatever it was against your name, you were dead sure it was different to everyone else's. Right ? "

It was a moment before Russell answered. There was never any point in lying to the old man. " So what ? You've got no room for a nervous system, Paul—you're too fat ! "

Sergeant's hands rose and fell with his steady breathing. " You're the best steerer I ever worked with, Gordy. But I'd like to see you with a pick and shovel. You'd be happier. Did you ever think how much we've earned together—not far short of three hundred thousand dollars. And what have *you* got out of it—a dozen suits and a guilty conscience! " He shook his head, eyes shut tight.

The hostess was working her way down, carrying a tray of drinks. Russell took his brandy, moodily searching for the right answer. A dozen times over the past couple of years, the old man had started something like this. A homily about the need to have purpose—Russell's guilt-complex. The implicit plug for an honest life was as much in keeping with Sergeant as a clergyman's collar.

They came casually, these needling suggestions, and always after a scene like the one at the airport. Criticism of his behaviour bothered Russell less than the sense of rejection.

" What do you propose I do with my money ? " he asked suddenly. " Start backing horses or get myself a daughter? "

Sergeant opened his eyes. " Ah, forget it, Gordy. Just keep finding a few more like that dame last year in Brussels. Twelve thousand dollars to start a model agency—*brother!* You could have *bought* a horse ! " He started to chuckle.

It was a sour memory. " And a daughter ? " asked Russell quietly.

Sergeant sat up very straight, his second chin bagging under his jaw. " You're right, son—Lucy's my problem. I've no business bothering you with it. When we get to Paris, we'll split this money down the middle. You go on down to the coast. We'll keep in touch and when Lucy's gone home we'll get back to work." The hand on his knee was freckled with age spots but steady.

Russell grinned. " What an old phony you are ! Is this trying to keep her away from my bad influence ? You know you couldn't last a day without me feeding you the right lines."

The old man was fond. " You'd hardly be her type. I've just had a thought, Gordy. Can you see what might worry that pilot more than losing his money ? "

Russell answered with conviction. " Nothing ! He's just a greedy mug."

Sergeant's eyes were shut. " And conceited, too—it's going to take him a while to get over the shock of being played for a sucker."

They dozed till a voice announced the imminent landing. It was two a.m. when the bus unloaded at the Quai d'Orsay. Another half-hour before they followed their bags into the hotel on the edge of the Bois de Boulogne.

They'd been using the Longchamps for years—whenever the money was right and they were in Paris. It was a small yet elegant establishment managed with discretion and efficiency. At the back was a tree-lined lane with a staff entrance. Here came such police visitors as there were. Their purpose nothing more sinister than the weekly collection of names for the *Contrôle des Étrangers*. The place had a cachet of respectability that was respected by the two con-men. They tipped adequately, avoided amatory scandal and kept their business at far remove.

The night clerk's greeting was courteous and mildly reproachful. " Welcome, gentlemen ! Your cable only arrived last night, M. Sergeant. For three rooms it is impossible. But we have one big room with two beds. Mademoiselle will be on the fifth floor overlooking the Bois.

M. Noget apologises—it is the best he could do at such short notice."

Sergeant was already filling in the *fiche*. Name, nationality, number of passport. The clerk handed him a blue envelope. " They sent this on from the air terminal."

Sergeant opened it hurriedly, his face expressionless as he scanned the contents.

When the door of the bedroom was closed, he gave the cable to Russell. " What do you make of this, Gordy ? "

Russell read the printed slip, yawning.

ARRIVE ORLY 14-05 PLEASE MEET ME STOP VERY WORRIED LOVE LUCY

The Canadian tried to hide his boredom. " It's a long way from California. She's a good girl. Will Pop meet me ? she asks." He shrugged. " It's normal."

Sergeant struggled short arms from his jacket. He snapped a catch on a bag and searched for pyjamas. He donned striped cotton, grunting with the effort. Finally, he carried the leather-framed photograph of his daughter to the dressing-table.

" All these years. Last time I saw her she still had a brace on her teeth. *You've* seen the vacation pictures she just sent. A grown woman ! "

Russell could have described pose and background in each coloured print. A dozen times his partner had insisted on their inspection. Lucy was a tall girl with straight blonde hair and a wide mouth. Whatever she was supposed to be doing was done with confidence. One picture showed her jumping a horse. Another had her in a group of skiers —snow-sprayed, leaning competently into a bend.

He snapped off the light button and crawled between his sheets. He lay for a long time, thinking about the man in the bed next to him. Sergeant rarely spoke of Lucy's mother. When he did, it was without like or dislike. Praise or criticism of her handling of his daughter was done dispassionately. Whatever had been between Sergeant and his wife was over. He asked no more of her than protection for his masquerade. It was a bargain in which she seemed to keep faith.

Russel turned on his side restlessly. The past hour had reversed the positions. Now it was Sergeant who looked to him for reassurance. Scared of facing the kid alone—concerned that his front of respectability might collapse—distressed most by the implications of his daughter's need of him. Lucy was going to be bad news—Russell was sure of it.

He spoke quietly into the darkness. "You're honking, Paul."

The strangled snores from the other bed continued. The snatched breathing of a man whose sleep is troubled.

The yellow-patterned curtains were bright with sunshine when Russell opened his eyes. He rolled easily, memory fitting circumstance to the surroundings. He must have slept heavily. A tray on the floor by his bed held cream, coffee, croissants. His watch on the bed-table showed a quarter past ten.

The bags had been unpacked. Through the open door of the commode, he saw his suits on hangers. A summer-weight jacket and trousers, freshly pressed, swung above his highly polished shoes.

Sergeant came into the room, dabbing at barbered cheeks. He started to knot a polka-dotted bow-tie. He wore blue with a plain white shirt. " You think before you start shooting off your mouth again about early rising." He dragged back the curtains, his mouth cheerful in the strong light. " The maid and the valet thought you looked cute ! "

Russell dipped the flaky cake into his coffee. " What about this airport business—you want me to be there ? "

Sergeant's quick move had the bedding off Russell. " You're damn' right, you'll be there ! We'll take a car out—wait lunch till we get Lucy back here."

Russell dressed with practised speed. Cool in the easy-fitting suit, he sat down on the edge of his bed. The first cigarette of the day bit his throat. " We'd better get this straight. I want to be word-perfect, Paul. You're an investment broker—I'm your assistant. The last four months, we've been in London on an assignment. Now why did we meet Lucy here ? "

Sergeant sat on the other bed. " We had an important appointment this morning in Paris. We'll drive Lucy to the bourse in a couple of days—it'll impress her. But don't forget, she's going to be too full of her own affairs to worry about ours. If you drop names, be sure they're ones we'll remember. This is my daughter—she's not a moron."

Russell looked at him carefully. Sergeant seemed far more relaxed. The Canadian nodded thoughtfully. "Maybe she's decided to come and live with you. Darn your socks and shake your martinis ! "

The suggestion left the old man untroubled. " You don't know her mother," he answered with feeling.

CHAPTER IV

WEDNESDAY A.M.

THE BIG PLANE circled the airfield, one tilted wing bright in the sunlight. Beneath, Orly was a patchwork of grey, green and silver. Watching it, Lucy Sergeant felt the window vibrating under her cheek. A black strip of highway pointed at the distant Paris skyline.

The florid man in the next seat hauled down a heavy dispatch-case, his gravel-throated voice cheerful.

" Well—this is it ! Another ten minutes and I'll have you off my hands."

She peered into the hand-mirror, drawing the red stick across her mouth. She rolled her lips carefully till the outline was even. She had noticed her neighbour for the first time at Idlewild. A bald prosperous-looking citizen coming across the hall followed by a chauffeur. He'd gone through pre-flight formalities with the patience of the experienced traveller. Once in the plane, he settled down with a sheaf of typescript.

She had been glad that he neither looked at her nor spoke. She was unable to control the hot shame of tears. Over the past two months, shock and the need to take decisions had left no time for weeping. The last few days in Monterey she remembered as a dream—the faces of people she'd known all her life, alive with small-town curiosity about her problem. Even the few who showed kindness were incapable of concealing implicit moral judgment. There was no escape from their interest. It had got so that people discussed her trip to Europe openly. The teller at the bank when she drew out the money to pay for her tickets— the girl at the Mission Travel Agency who sold them. It had been Mr. Leonard at the Western Union office who delivered Monterey's last word. He read out her cable to her father in a slow drawl and wiped the tobacco stains from the edge of his mouth.

" So you're off to Europe, Lucy." It was an indictment in itself. Ignoring the clattering machine behind him, he leaned both elbows on the counter. " It's a pity your pa couldn't be with you at a time like this. Not that anybody can do much to help you. You gotta pray for guidance, Lucy. That's what me and Mrs. Leonard said way back last fall. And a lot of Christian people will be praying with you."

She had tucked the cable into her jeans. Her voice was steady. " Are you including Mrs. Leonard's brother ? If you are, for the town drunk he's got his nerve ! "

The sense of injustice she had as she climbed aboard the San Francisco express lasted as far as New York. Not till she was safely on the plane did the taut fabric of self-control collapse. The tears had been incidental. Foremost in her mind was the certainty of relief. A few more hours and her troubles would be shared, if not over. It was the moment the man sitting next to her chose for his gesture of understanding. She made nervous repairs to her face then accepted the cigarette he gave her. For an hour he encouraged her to talk, ignoring both tears and their cause.

With a complete stranger it seemed easier to talk. Most of what she said was about her father—creating a picture of respectability and success that gave her interior satisfaction.

Now the plane went into a long, flat dive. She braced her legs against the shock of landing. " You've been very kind to me, Mr. Wontner. You'll have to give my father the chance of thanking you."

The wheels of the plane jarred twice then grabbed traction on the tarmac. Turning on to a diagonal runway, the pilot taxied to a stop in front of the main airport building.

Wontner's panama bore a gay band. He touched a hand to it. " I'll be delighted. A man with a daughter like you deserves congratulating ! "

She was in the van of passengers as they walked towards the customs hall. People were hanging over the rails of the observation platform—a jumble of down-turned faces dotted with dark glasses. Suppose her father hadn't received her cable—worse—suppose something had stopped his coming to Paris. She clutched her purse and passport, staying close to Wontner. She was through customs before she saw the man waiting by the barrier. The image she'd kept of her father was sharp. This plump elegant man seemed much older. Her run carried her into his arms. For a moment she was content to stay there without speaking —the smell of tobacco and face-lotion a link with her childhood.

Sergeant held her at length. " Come on—let me get a good look at you ! "

Wontner was waiting a few feet away, his hat in hand. She smiled happily, caught in sudden comradeship. "Daddy —this is Mr. Wontner. He's put up with me all the way from New York. I wasn't the best seat companion."

The two men shook hands, their exchange of regard curious. Wontner's voice was pleasant. " Pay no attention

to her, Mr. Sergeant. You have a very lovely daughter—
I'm glad to have had the chance of meeting her."

She wanted her father to break the silence. " Mr.
Wontner's staying in Paris, Daddy," she prompted.

Sergeant's grip on her arm was proprietorial. " Ah yes,
of course. You must have a meal with us, Mr. Wontner.
You're on a business trip I take it ? "

A uniformed driver took Wontner's baggage slips. The
American nodded. " That's right. From what Lucy's
been telling me we might even have some interests in
common. I understand you're in investment brokerage ?
Give me a ring—I'm at the Crillon. May I give you a lift
into Paris ? " He nodded after his chauffeur.

The warmth of her father's arm was good about her body.
She stood close to him, suddenly secure. " We've got a car
here," said Sergeant. " Thanks again for your kindness to
Lucy. I'll certainly give you a ring."

They stood for a moment, watching Wontner to the big
glass doors. He turned as he went out, flourishing his hat
in farewell.

A younger man came over to join them. He was brown-
haired and sunburned. " This is Gordy Russell, my
assistant, Lucy," said her father.

She smiled acknowledgment. The Canadian's hand-
clasp was right—firm yet fleeting. " I've heard enough
about Mr. Russell to recognise him. In Daddy's letters,
it's usually ' my boy, Gordy ' ! "

Russell shrugged. " You should hear him at the end of
a bad trading day—he's not quite so quaint." He held out
a hand. " If you give me the baggage checks I'll have
your stuff brought out to the car."

She was searching her bag, fumbling in her haste. " Try
your pockets," Russell suggested.

She found the Canadian's manner neither hostile nor
superior. Yet his complete assurance made her nervous.
She gave him the numbered checks gratefully.

In the car, she sat between them, her father's voice a
comforting background to her thoughts. That last night

at home, she'd walked out alone to Cypress Point. The twisted trees at the edge of the golf links were black in the moonlight. No more than a few yards away, the ocean sucked at the deserted beach. A few lights shone from the lodge.

Chin huddled on her knees, she'd sat listening to the bark of a seal from the seabound rocks in front of her. Then, this meeting with her father had seemed so easy. How many times over the years had she written out her troubles—counting the days till the answer would be dropped through the mail-box. The long thin envelopes with the familiar handwriting bore the certainty of understanding. This fear of being rejected had to be false. It was she who had changed, not her father.

She gripped his arm fiercely, seeking assurance in the physical contact.

" Daddy ! "

He turned quickly, holding her hand captive against his side. " What is it, Lucy ? "

She shook her head, looking straight in front of her, " Nothing—just that ! "

Russell crossed and uncrossed his legs. " What sort of night did you have in New York ? "

The tension in her body eased. " The airline booked a room for me on the East Side. I was in bed at nine, listening to the gulls and tugs on the river." The rest of it—the endless review of events lasting into the small hours of morning—was better forgotten.

The interest in her father's voice was forced and stilted. " How's your mother ? "

She kept her tone casual. " Fine—just green with envy at me over this trip." She shut her eyes, willing Sergeant to drop the subject.

Russell cut in, inviting her to follow the sweep of his arm. The car was circling the vastness of the Place de la Concorde. In front of them was the long lovely line of the Champs-Élysées, the triumphal arch at its end silhouetted against the sky.

" Our hotel's just beyond that," said Russell. " Your room overlooks the park. A summer day in Paris, Lucy. Does it come up to expectation ? "

He'd taken over the conversation almost as if he sensed her anxiety. She moved her head. " It's wonderful. Those tiny bridges over the river. The shops, the trees. It's all too much for a small-town girl but it's wonderful. Everything ! "

He was mock-serious. " That's a pretty wide statement, you know ! "

She found herself really looking at him for the first time. His head at the back was flat—the hair much longer than they wore it in California. She guessed doubtfully at his age. The grey over his ears was offset by the way he moved. It was hard to say if he was thirty or forty. Certainly somewhere in between.

" I'll include you," she said gravely.

Sergeant's tone was tolerant. " Don't let this character fool you, Lucy. The Canadian charm gets switched on regularly. Whenever he meets a pretty girl, in fact." His round face was thoughtful. " The Crillon, Wontner said— you'll find that a little different from the hotel we're going to, honey. The way the European investment market has been lately, I've been cutting overheads. I've got too much capital tied up in stock at the moment. Don't worry— we'll still be able to send you home with some Paris dresses." His hand was warm on hers.

She forced herself to look through the car window, fighting the lump in her throat. Beyond the spread of chestnut trees, the park rolled to a shimmer of water. A solitary horse-rider was jogging along the bridle path. The car turned into a forecourt that fronted a thin elegant building. Striped awnings protected portico and windows. The *chasseur* had his white-gloved hand on the door handle.

Russell helped her out. " Home," he said pleasantly. " Complete with an Empire telephone and garlicked chambermaids."

She stood at the reception desk, bright-eyed as people

fussed over her. Sergeant's voice cut through the confusion. " They'll show you your room, honey. The girl does your unpacking. We'll meet you down here in a half-hour's time, for lunch."

She followed the page into the elevator. Upstairs, he pulled the cord on the curtains. It was a gay feminine room with angled mirrors. The boy threw open the door to the bathroom and ran hot water in a hand-basin.

" *À votre service, mademoiselle* ! "

She pushed a dollar bill at him and sat down on the bed. A giant bowl of roses was on the night table, their scent sweet and heady. The propped card was printed in ink.

WELCOME TO PARIS, LUCY.

Smiling, she picked up the phone and called her father's room.

CHAPTER V

WEDNESDAY P.M.

FOR A SECOND the instrument hung between Sergeant's thumb and forefinger. He cradled it thoughtfully. "Flowers ! Somebody's sent Lucy flowers and she thinks it was me."

Russell was lolling at the window, cleaning his nails. " What of it," he asked idly. " It happens, even with fathers ! "

Sergeant blinked. " That was a pleasant thing to do, Gordy."

Russell tossed the nail-file at the dressing-table. His voice was ironical. " A pleasure. It's that Canadian charm you were talking about. All those women in my life—I've got the habit." He used his hairbrush with vigour, talking into the mirror. " She looks pretty edgy to me, Paul.

Why don't the two of you have lunch alone ? She won't want to talk in front of me."

Sergeant shook his head with decision. " She's got to have time to unwind. She'll talk when she's ready—whether you're there or not ! "

Anything to avoid the issue, thought Russell. They were involved in yet another con trick. The girl was no less a mark than the pilot in London. Only for Sergeant at least the stakes were higher now.

He crossed the room. The bed sank under his weight. His tone was deliberately hard. " Look, Paul—have you thought that she might be going to find her news tough to break to *any* man ? Even a doctor."

Sergeant turned quickly, the set of his face hostile. " What's that supposed to mean ? "

Russell lifted his shoulders. " You *know* what it's supposed to mean ! A small town's no place to have a child unless there's a husband to go with it."

Sergeant's face was shocked. He spoke in a whisper. " No. No, you're wrong, Gordy. Lucy's a . . ."

" A *what* ? " Russell broke in impatiently. " O.K.—she's your daughter. They're *all* somebody's daughter. She's still a woman. Suppose——" he parried the interruption. " I said *suppose* I'm right, Paul ! That po-faced expression you're wearing isn't going to give her much hope."

It didn't matter what either of them believed—just as long as Sergeant would accept the possibilities. He flicked the ash from his jacket. " Read your Freud, Paul. He says a lot on the subject of father and daughter. It seems that even being a long-distance father changes nothing ! "

Sergeant climbed up carefully. He stood with his head cocked like that of some apprehensive bird. " I'll talk to her at dinner to-night. But there's something *you* ought to remember—it could be as much your problem as Lucy's. What you do is less important than the way you feel about it afterwards." His smile was without malice. " I don't know whether you'll find that in Freud."

They ate by the side of the fountain in the shady courtyard.

A dozen times, Russell found himself watching the girl speculatively. She had changed to a belted white tunic dress and sandals. She wore no jewellery other than a sturdy strap watch. The inevitable sling-bag was at her feet. Miss Monterey, 1961, he thought. There'd be fifty like her on Del Monte Avenue, any summer evening. Cool, self-assured and American. Yet here she was, sitting with a couple of con-men, six thousand miles from home. Hidden somewhere beneath that smooth wrap of hair was the reason.

He watched as Sergeant paid the cheque. The older man never used money as a weapon to bludgeon a servant. For four months he'd been tapped-out yet he could still hand over the folded bill without haste or loss to the *maître d'hôtel's* dignity. Odd. This same urbane skill Sergeant had in handling the public seemed to desert him once faced with Lucy.

Lunch over, they walked five blocks to the crowded Champs-Élysées. The tables in front of Fouquet's were jammed with tourists. A hand on his daughter's elbow, Sergeant steered her forward. Russell was careful not to show his amusement. The old boy was really putting on a show for her. A bribed waiter whisked chairs from astonished patrons—materialised a table and forced it into a corner near the sidewalk. Lucy sat between the two men.

Sergeant stripped the band from his cigar, leaning over to catch the flame that Russell extended. He leaned back, plumply content, exhorting his daughter between exhalations.

" This is what you read about back home, honey. This sidewalk's a walking gossip column. If you sit here long enough you'll see 'em all. Dukes—bums—and Hollywood expatriates."

The match had burned low in Russell's fingers. He dropped it carefully into the ash-tray. He got up without haste to smile down at them both.

" I'll be right back—you'll excuse me ! "

Beyond the hurrying waiter, Slezak was shoving his way through the tables, heading directly for them.

He caught up an empty chair, carrying it like a battering ram. It was too late for Russell to divert the pilot's attention.

Slezak halted, leaning both hands on the back of his chair. He greeted both men with the ease of an old friend, using no names, then sat down uninvited. He was wearing the same suit and was hatless. Stubble sprouted on chin and cheeks. His eyes were both tired and hostile. The close-cropped head was even yellower in the sunlight. He sat staring at the girl, his big hands playing with Russell's pack of cigarettes.

"Well, here's a surprise," he said casually.

The expression on Sergeant's face had not changed but his cheeks were pasty. Russell sat down again. The first shock of Slezak's arrival was over—only stomach-crawling fear remained. The American showed no sign of leaving. In a minute, he'd yell for the police and a flying wedge of waiters would arrive at the gallop. Sergeant's mouth was moving without sound—as if trying over some formula that might save him from disgrace.

Slezak's appraisal of the girl was slow. "They don't seem to want me to know you—I'm Stan Slezak!"

Russell's hands were gripping the edge of the iron table. A brawl could save nothing. His voice was even. "This is Lucy Sergeant, Paul's daughter."

"Paul's daughter, eh!" Slezak's disbelieving production of the words was just short of insult.

The girl flushed. "You sound surprised, Mr. Slezak. Perhaps it's a relationship that bothers you!"

"Perhaps," agreed Slezak. He was unmoved by her anger, content to command the situation.

A woman at the next table turned her head as if sensible to the tension. Russell got to his feet again. "I'd like a word with you alone, Slezak." He jerked a hand at the interior of the restaurant. Seconds ticked off in his head as the American looked from one to the other.

"O.K." Slezak's regard levelled on the girl. "Don't run away—I only just got here."

Inside, the two men stood at the empty bar. Russell moved between Slezak and the door. With any sort of luck, Sergeant would use the break to hustle the girl away. He took a quick look over his shoulder, hope dying. They were still at the table.

Slezak grinned. "That's a nice hotel you've found yourselves. Right on the park. A great position for handing out charity. What'll you do—start a soup kitchen there for the people you've swindled?"

Russell wet his lips. "Suppose we cut out the grand-standing. If you're going to holler for the police, go ahead. It isn't going to get your money back!"

Waiters hurried through the service doors, indifferent to the two men at the unattended bar. Slezak leaned back against a pillar. "I guess you know more about Scotland Yard than I do—that's a pretty efficient organisation they've got! It was ten o'clock when I reached there—it took 'em a quarter of an hour to find your picture from my description."

The Canadian moved to the bar, lighting a cigarette. Something didn't jell. It took no more than minutes for the Yard to put out a HOLD notice in every sea and airport in the U.K. Yet he and Paul had come through.

"A man there called Brace seems to know you pretty well," said Slezak. "It turns out you're quite an operator."

Russell's voice was perfectly steady. "That makes a pair of us. What was that bit about a security officer?"

Slezak waved away the remark. His tone was mild. "Oh, that. But I didn't break any law. Let's get back to the point. I'll tell you what I said to your friend the cop when he showed me your picture. 'No, Officer. I don't think this is the man who robbed me!'" He shifted his weight from one foot to the other. "They were pretty disappointed up there. This guy Brace made it plain that if I ever changed my mind he'd be glad to hear from me."

Russell ground a heel on his cigarette butt. "So you're

Dick Tracy. I don't know what your angle is, Slezak, but you can be sure of this. Lay off Sergeant and his daughter and I'll see you get your dough back."

Slezak's square, blond head lowered a little. " I'm getting to that. *I'll* make the conditions ! I want you to hear the rest of it. Maybe you're not as smart as you imagine. I had your real name—right ? So I tried to figure out what I'd do in your place. Passenger Inquiries helped out. I reached London Airport twenty minutes after your flight took off. And when you got here, you left an address in case a cable came to the terminal. Don't you think I've got friends there ? " He shook his head. " Sucker ! "

Russell shifted his feet, looking at the other man cautiously. " Well, come on—what exactly is it you want ? "

Slezak took him by the arm again, his mouth hard. " Don't be so tough with me, Mac ! We're going to be buddies, the four of us. You—the girl, Sergeant and me ! I always heard guys like you kept their women out of the rackets."

Russell freed himself from the other's grip. He spoke with quiet deliberation. " Keep your hands off me—I've told you once—this is Sergeant's daughter."

Slezak laughed till his eyes watered. His expression changed suddenly. " I want you and Sergeant downstairs in your hotel lobby at six o'clock. Without the girl." He started for the door then stopped. " If something keeps you, you'll find me at the British Embassy, filing charges ! "

He led the way back to the table, square-backed and smiling. He bent solicitously over Lucy. " It was a conversation you wouldn't have enjoyed." He raised a hand in farewell.

They watched the towering blond head till it disappeared. Russell massaged his left ear furiously, a working signal that immediate danger was over.

The girl frowned, the pattern of freckles changing round her eyes. " I'm afraid Mr. Slezak's manners would get him into a lot of trouble in Monterey."

Sergeant called for the cheque. "I'm sorry, honey. In my business you can't pick your associates. He's a very useful man, wouldn't you say, Gordy?" The old man's eyes were anxious.

Russell held the girl's chair. He looked over her shoulder at his partner. "I'll give you the answer on that one at six o'clock!"

Back at the hotel, Slezak was lolling in a hammock in the courtyard. The interval had been used to advantage. His suit was freshly pressed and he had shaved. He waved in a friendly way as they crossed the yard.

Sergeant took his room key from the clerk. A folded message was with it. He passed the note to his daughter. "It's your friend from the plane—he wants us to lunch with him to-morrow. Would you like that?"

She nodded. Sergeant gave her her key. "Get some rest, honey. You want to feel good for to-night."

She slung the strap of her bag across her shoulder. Her head was down so that her expression was hidden. "I thought I might get a chance to talk to you."

Sergeant lifted her chin. "You will—we're going to have a quiet meal together. Gordy's out on the town."

She looked at Russell speculatively. "There's plenty for me to do—but I don't need rest. I'm not as fragile as you think!"

Once upstairs, Sergeant shut the door of their room. He exploded into a rush of questions. "What's that clown doing here, Gordy—how in hell did he get here?"

Russell ran himself a glass of cold water, washed down the bitter aspirins. What fear he still felt was mixed with excitement. His account of the talk with Slezak was followed without interruption. Sergeant drummed nervous fingers then delivered his verdict quietly. "We've got to get rid of him, Gordy. You were right about him. But what's he want? Why hasn't he gone to the cops here— *why*, Gordy?"

Russell pulled aside the window curtain. The top of Slezak's head showed above the swing chair below. "Let's find out," the Canadian said quickly. "Why wait till six o'clock ? "

Sergeant shrugged plump shoulders. Russell took the phone. "There's a gentleman sitting in the courtyard—a Mr. Slezak. That's right, wearing a blue suit. Will you ask him to come up to the room ? "

He watched from the window as Slezak followed the page into the hotel. In a couple of minutes there was a knock at the door. Russell opened. Slezak made an entrance relaxed to the point of condescension. He sprawled on Russell's bed, linking his hands behind his neck, grinning up at Sergeant. "Well, now, Mr. Clancy."

Russell cut in. "All right, Slezak—you've made your point. Now suppose you tell us what you want."

Slezak raised himself on an elbow, ignoring the Canadian's outburst. He spoke to Sergeant. "Don't you ever muzzle this guy ? All this tough talk—you're a couple of con-men —not killers ! "

Sergeant shrugged, his whole body indicating a sporting acceptance of defeat. "You're an intelligent man—try to understand our position. We've been at this racket a long time—out of the blue we run into someone who outsmarts us. Do you expect us to act normally ? "

Slezak straightened up and lit a cigarette. The flattery implicit in Sergeant's speech seemed to please him. "I read a book on the plane coming over. Some British cop wrote it. He claims that to fall for a con-trick, you have to have larceny in your heart." He tapped himself on the chest, spiralling smoke from the corner of his mouth. "I have it."

Sergeant nodded understanding. "Most people do. I'm going to make a guess," he said shrewdly. "What you want is your money back and something on top—is that right ? "

Russell watched in silence, content with Sergeant as spokesman.

Slezak swung his feet to the ground, rubbing the top of his head ruefully. "Right *and* wrong. *I'll* tell you something. I was fired yesterday for smuggling—no trouble with the cops but I'll never fly again."

Sergeant's eyes were hidden in fat pouches. " So you want your money back and a dividend—is that it ? "

Slezak's affability vanished—eyes and mouth were implacable. " Let's treat the money you took from me as a fee for training. I've got to understand every move in this racket. And when you find the next victim the pay-off will have to be big enough for the three of us."

Russell's short laugh stabbed at the other's vanity. "What do you think we're running—a kindergarten for con-men ? There isn't a mark out of captivity who wouldn't have you pegged as a liar from the off."

Slezak shrugged. " Like you, for instance ? The only thing you could see last night was my money. Everything I told you about myself, you believed. Anyone outside your little club's a sucker. That's what you think, isn't it ! You're forgetting the most important factor. I'm *here*— giving the instructions."

Sergeant bustled between them. " Nobody's denying it. Only things are more complicated than you imagine. I've got a daughter upstairs. She thinks I'm an honest man. It's got to stay that way for another week, then we'll talk business."

Slezak looked back at him coolly. " There's a cottage by the town dump in Sheboygan. A little white-haired lady sits there knitting spaghetti—my mother ! We'll keep the women out of it. You want to tell this doll you're a minister of the gospel, I've no objections. I won't louse up your story. But we'll start for the big money as of now." He swung his big body on Russell. " You'll be my tutor, Mac. For your sake I hope I grow to like you better." He took hold of Russell's wrist. " Here, at eleven o'clock to-morrow morning. We'll have the first lesson." He went out leaving the door to the corridor wide open.

Russell kneaded his wrist, his voice rough. " I'm going out to Doc Springer's place. He's got some of these Left

Bank Algerians on call. A thousand bucks will put this bastard in a barrel of cement."

Sergeant pitched his cigar butt in the lavatory bowl. "Now you listen to me! The guy was right—we're conmen, not killers. Slezak's forgetting one thing——" His face was thoughtful.

Russell looked up quickly. "What's that?"

Sergeant spread his hands. "As things are, all he's got to do is make a phone call and we're both in the Santé Prison. But once he's turned a trick with us, he's got nothing left. He's in the same position as we are. That's when we dump him!"

CHAPTER VI

WEDNESDAY P.M.

SHE LAY in the deep tub till the water grew tepid. A nearby clock boomed six as she started to dress for dinner. The desire to look her best persisted in spite of her anxiety. All her cotton dresses seemed too jazzy for dinner in Paris. The grey-flannel frock she had bought in San Francisco would be warm but it would pass any test. White braid on the round standaway collar was reproduced at the hem of the belled skirt. The skirt was fashionably short but she wasn't worried about her legs. White shoes and clutch-purse completed the outfit. Now she was ready to use the small bottle of scent as her mother had taught her. Wrist-pulse, temple and throat. Making sure that she had Doctor Schulze's letter, she shut the bedroom door behind her.

As she left the elevator, a voice hailed her from the gilt-backed sofa.

"Over here, Lucy! Your father's still having trouble with his bow-tie."

Russell waited till she was seated. His look was frankly

appreciative. "Very pretty. I don't mean only the dress but Miss Sergeant."

She found it difficult not to sound coy. She murmured thanks, taking the cigarette he offered. This man's face showed what he felt. At Fouquet's that afternoon, she'd seen the hostility and wariness when that bore accosted them. Now the Canadian's smile was friendly.

"I thought you were out on the town," she said lightly.

He blew out the match. "What you really want to know is whether you're dining alone with your father!"

She let smoke trickle from her mouth. It was hard to tell if his presence would embarrass her. But at least she was bound to her father by blood and affection. This man she didn't know. She used his name deliberately, unwilling to reject the comradeship he inspired. "I don't mean to be rude, Gordy. What I have to say to Daddy isn't easy—I hope you'll make allowances for that."

He took her cigarette away gently and dropped it in an ash-tray. His voice was quiet. "I want you to listen to me, Lucy. In many ways Paul's like a father to me, too. I don't want to see him hurt." He silenced her protest determinedly. "There are two things I want you to remember. Paul's over sixty and cares for nothing except your happiness. As long as you remember that, you'll find me a good friend. Whatever's between the pair of you is none of my business."

She moved nervously, her bag clattering to the floor. She watched as he bent to retrieve it, disturbed by the force of his sincerity. His manner was a challenge. As though he was preparing for her defection.

He laid the bag in her lap. "No hard feelings, Lucy?"

She shook her head. "Of course not. But *I'm* fond of my father, too, you know!" The smile robbed the words of malice.

He climbed to his feet. "Fair enough. Can we keep this conversation between us? I don't think your father would appreciate it."

The implication of a common understanding pleased her.

"I won't say anything," she promised. "Have a swell evening!"

She could still see him as he waited for a cab in the courtyard. For a while she sat on the sofa, conscious of a sense of loss yet uncertain of its reason.

The restaurant her father had chosen was on the Boulevard St. Germain. They ate outside, hidden from the sidewalk by a screen of shrubs. A thin violinist wandered about the tables with half-shut eyes, indifferent to everything save his Magyar music.

Once or twice she had been on the verge of stumbling into her tale. Each time her father stopped her. When the coffee was poured, he shifted the small lamp so that her face was left in shadow. His voice was warm and he smiled at her. "Nothing's going to change us, Lucy. Nothing!"

She sat very straight, hearing unfamiliar sounds. The rapid beauty of the foreign language—the absence of blaring horns on the boulevard—the sadness of the fiddle tune. A strange background to a sordid little tale, she thought. She spoke at the red glow of her father's cigar. "You asked me about my mother. I told you a lie. She's sick. Desperately sick." The words came in spasms and not as she had rehearsed them. "It's drink. She started three years ago. I wanted to tell you then but Doctor Schulze said no. It was only the change of life, he said. She'd get better." Across the table her father's cigar burned steadily. "She got worse. Ever since I was twelve, she's been like a sister rather than a mother." She realised that there was no hope of translating the vivid memory. "Now I've had to watch her turn into a hostile stranger who'll do anything to get drink. Even to lying and stealing. That's how it ended—she stole a bottle of whisky from the liquor store last January and was arrested."

Her father's voice was shocked. "God Almighty, Lucy! Where is she now?"

"At home. They gave her a suspended sentence— remanded to Doctor Schulze's care. After the first shock was over, it meant nothing to her. It all started again.

Hiding bottles in the house. If I touched them, she said I was like the others—trying to kill her."

Sergeant's hands cradled hers swiftly. "You were crazy not to tell me before. Now we've got to work something out. One thing's certain—you can't go back there."

She shook her head wearily. "You don't understand, Daddy. She's still my mother."

"Then what?" he asked.

She unfastened her bag. He brought the lamp nearer, reading the letter she gave him. After a while he looked up. "The Mayo Clinic! Do you have any idea how much that would cost? And who in hell *is* Doctor Schulze?"

She blinked. "We've known him ever since I can remember. It seems as though Mother set out to destroy every friendship we had. Doctor Schulze was the last. Now there's nothing more that he can do. The specialist in San Francisco says it's her last chance. It would mean at least two years in the clinic." She moved her shoulders hopelessly. "Whatever happens—whether you'll help her or not—I've got to be with her." She wiped the corners of her eyes and packed lipstick and mirror carefully into her purse. "I'd better go back to the hotel, Daddy," she said quietly. "I'm sorry."

He came with her as far as her door. Outside he held her very close. She had the sudden urge to take his head on her breast. As though his was the greater need of comfort.

He spoke with difficulty. "Try to get some sleep, darling. Whatever happens, I'm going to help you."

Russell had been back at the hotel for more than an hour. He lay on the bed, ears tuned to the drone of the elevator—the rumble of the cage door as it opened and shut. He snapped on the bedside lamp as the key turned in the lock.

Sergeant lowered himself into a chair. He sat, weeping like an old man, hopelessly and without sound.

Russell waited till the fit was over. "What is it, Paul?" Compassion changed to indignation as he listened.

The defencelessness of a man whose courage had been

his own strength shocked him. He took the letter Sergeant gave him. The guarded phrasing of two medical opinions was without impact.

" The Mayo Clinic for two years ! What do these guys think you are ! Have you any idea what a thing like this would cost, Paul ? "

Sergeant undressed as if each movement was a struggle. His voice was tired but under control. " Twelve thousand dollars, maybe—I dunno." He went into the bathroom.

Russell climbed from his bed searching the drawer for an unopened packet of cigarettes. As yet his anger had no focal point and needed one. The girl upstairs—that was too easy. She was no more responsible for Sergeant's distress than a postman who carries a court summons. He watched the old man get into his bed, then sat down beside him. " I shouldn't bother—with any luck, your wife's drinking herself to death right now. It'll be cheaper than the clinic."

Sergeant shook his head. " Lucy thinks I've got the money. Why shouldn't she—I've been conning her for years ! I've promised I'll help, Gordy. If I don't, it's the end of me with her. I know it."

Sergeant's teeth had been left in the bathroom. His face was unfamiliar and grotesque. Russell looked at him with affection. " What do we do, Pop ? " he asked quietly. " You say it."

" Find the money ! " The flat statement was without compromise.

" Just like that ? " Russell was patient. " You know I'm with you, Paul. But you're losing your sense of proportion. Last night in London we had a chance in a million. This is Paris in the heart of the tourist season. There are fifty grafters out looking for mugs. We could spend months looking for one."

The old man's expression was obstinate. " We're going to get this money, Gordy—and get it fast ! "

Russell paced nervously. Suddenly he turned, flicking his fingers, inspired. Enthusiasm gave his voice conviction.

" Of course, Wontner ! He's made to order. What we need is speed—right ? Well, Lucy's already saved us half the steering. She's established two things for you—you're wealthy and you're respectable."

It seemed a long time before Sergeant answered. He ground his knuckles into the white upstanding hair. " That's out, Gordy. Lucy mustn't be involved in any of this."

Russell poked a finger at the old man's chest. " You're out of your mind, Paul. Lucy's in it up to her neck already. You're meeting Wontner at the Crillon to-morrow—suppose some cop who knows you was there. You'd lose Wontner —you'd make no money and Lucy would *still* be involved. Listen—we can beat him somewhere else—move him to Brussels or the coast. Lucy will be in no danger. She needs the dough, doesn't she ? "

" It's the principle," said Sergeant obstinately. " We'll do it some other way."

Russell shook his head. " Principle, yet ! Christ, Paul, you must like punishment. O.K., we'll do it some other way."

He cut the light and got back into bed. Sergeant's behaviour worried him. First his partner went to pieces under emotional strain. Now came this lunatic insistence on doing the impossible the hard way. Russell turned suddenly, his voice sharp with memory. " Paul, we're not off the hook till Slezak's completely involved—you said it yourself a couple of hours ago. How's he supposed to fit into a quick score ? " He stared into the darkness, sure that Sergeant was awake. But there was no answer.

The wheel of his thoughts slowly gathered speed. The coup they'd pulled with Slezak had been both crude and simple. The old-timers were right—the Hot Seat was no more ambitious than larceny from the person. But the kind of money they were going for now required finesse, skill, and split-second timing.

To play The Rag successfully, you needed three men. Any other time, Sergeant would have recruited some free-lance from the pool of grafters always in Paris. Now

Slezak had to be third man. Memory took a hop from the pilot to Lucy. The Canadian settled himself for sleep, uncomfortably aware that she had succeeded in making her problem his own.

CHAPTER VII

THURSDAY A.M.

SLEZAK HAD been sitting in the Bois since six that morning. Though the early sun held no heat as yet, he dragged his chair to the shade of a tree facing the hotel. From time to time, he inspected the canopied windows, defeated by the anonymity of drawn curtains. There was no way of telling which was the girl's room, which was Sergeant's.

Last night, he'd watched the three of them leaving the hotel. The pairing intrigued him. First the Canadian off on a brief and solitary excursion. Then the old man and Lucy. Everything added to Slezak's certainty. Whatever the reason for the " father and daughter " bit, the relationship was phony.

He kept his eyes on the hotel entrance, his mind returning to Brace's office at Scotland Yard. The detective had made one thing plain. Russell and Sergeant were important operators. International thieves capable of making the long hop from country to country with as little fuss as a store clerk boarding his bus. It wouldn't be difficult with a good-looking girl as a front.

There was a high-pitched whistle from the courtyard across the way. A cab pulled from the line. He moved his chair a foot, watching the baggage being loaded into the cab. Two elderly women climbed after it and he relaxed. He'd left the two men the night before, certain that as soon as he was gone they'd be at work on a scheme to screw him up. It was logical. Sergeant's age and experience made his behaviour predictable. The Canadian represented the unknown quantity, in spite of the older man's apparent control. Later that night, the weakness of his scheme hit Slezak. It would be no trick for the men and the girl to get out of Paris—either together or separately.

Slezak's vigil had started just before seven the previous evening. A call in the early hours of the morning to the hotel desk assured him that there was no indication of the trio's departure. A few hours' rest had given him his answer. Now he had the means to plug the hole.

He walked across the street. Breakfast was in the small room adjoining the lobby. From his table he had a clear view of both stairway and elevator. It was gone eight when he started up the stairs. The door to Sergeant's room was closed. The key in the lock made a survey impossible. He used his knuckles to rap.

" Who is it ? "

He recognised the Canadian's voice. " Slezak," he answered. Nothing happened. He thudded noisily with the heel of his fist.

The door opened and he pushed his way in. The two men were fully dressed—the remains of their breakfast littering the beds.

The Canadian scowled. " Eleven o'clock, you said."

Slezak locked the door again, pocketing the key. He leaned against the dressing-table. " I changed my mind. I was worried in case you thought of leaving without saying good-bye."

Sergeant cleared his throat. " Leaving ! See here, Stan—we settled this yesterday, I thought."

Russell looked from the locked door to Slezak. " Ah, let him be, Paul. He's still playing cops and robbers."

A folded slip of paper was on top of the dressing-table. From the corner of an eye, Slezak saw that it was written on hotel stationery. He eased his body, pocketing the message.

" I want both your passports," he said steadily. " You'll get them back when they're needed. From now on, *I* buy the tickets whenever we move. We'll forget the girl's—

she's not likely to go far without Father." He grinned across the room.

Sergeant blinked fast. " This is senseless. You're way out of line, Stan ! I told you last night—we're ready to do business—there's nothing else we *can* do. Put yourself in our place."

Slezak went as far as the window. He showed them the door key in his palm. " I have. That's why I'm taking the passports. You guys take a lot of convincing. In two minutes this key goes through the window. When the chambermaid lets us out, I call the cops." He turned his wrist, watching the moving second hand.

Sergeant fumbled his passport from a drawer. " Do what the man says," he instructed wearily.

The two documents made a comforting bulge in Slezak's pocket. He tossed the room key to Russell. " I thought you'd see it my way. Now, listen—I told you I need money fast—I meant it. How long's it going to take me to learn what's necessary. A day—three days ? "

Sergeant's forehead was damp. " You've seen us work, Slezak. There's no easy way to learn."

Slezak looked at each man in turn. " I've paid for the best tuition. I'm going to see that I get it."

Russell turned the key in the door. " Why don't you tell him the truth, Paul ! "

" Suppose *you* tell me," invited Slezak.

The Canadian leant his back against the wall. " You've got one thing in your favour—you're a natural liar. Maybe you're capable of doing somebody else besides Dick Tracy —I dunno. But if you're half as smart as you think you are, I could have you ready in three days. And if we have a mark in three months, we'll be lucky ! " He met Slezak's scrutiny unmoved.

Slezak was alert to the implication in the Canadian's last words. The guy was playing for safety. This pair could make sure they found no victim for three months. They'd gamble on his dwindling interest to get them off the hook. Either that or rob half a dozen people without him being the wiser. He signalled Russell to open the door.

"I'll give it a week," he said briefly. "After that I'll be bored." He followed Russell into the corridor.

They sat by the tree that had been his vantage point. A couple of hundred yards away, the Métro station emptied itself of office workers at regular intervals. The wide avenues radiating from the Arc de Triomphe were already jammed with traffic. Overhead the sun had climbed in a cloudless sky, spreading its warmth on grass, trees and water. Occasionally, a woman's heels clicked by on the hidden sidewalk —a policeman's whistle sounded in peremptory rebuke. Apart from these intrusions the park was still peaceful.

Slezak yawned. They had sat in silent hostility for fully five minutes. He tipped his chair back against the giant chestnut tree.

"What do you say we stop acting like a couple of kids? Whether we like it or not, we're going to see a lot of one another!"

The Canadian shrugged. "You've got my passport in your pocket. You've threatened to holler copper twice in the last twelve hours—what do you want from me—handstands?"

Slezak switched the blade of grass from one corner of his mouth to the other. "A little common sense, maybe. I want to get your point of view. What have you got against me? Suppose I'd robbed you—what would you have done?"

Russell dug a heel into the turf. "If you beat me on merit, nothing," he said shortly.

Slezak's voice was still amiable. "Isn't that exactly what I *have* done? Merit's where you find it. Let me ask you something. What made you pick on me in the first place? Is it manner or appearance? Just what the hell is it that gives you the signal?"

Russell's head was bent. He seemed to give the question full consideration. Finally, he looked up, his eyes serious.

"I'll put it on the line, Slezak. You say you want to

use us to make a score. You're holding all the cards. As
far as I'm concerned, you're in. But when we work, you'll
do as you're told—the same as I will. Only one man gives
the orders—Paul ! "

Slezak tilted forward. " Fair enough. I want this deal
to be soon and safe. It'll be my first and last. Now answer
my question—what do you look for in a mark in the first
place ? "

Russell swung round to face him. Some of the Canadian's
hostility appeared to have gone. " You can't put a terrier's
nose on a sheep-dog. I do the finding. Worry about *your*
end of the business. We'll start as of now. Think yourself
into believing what I'm telling you—your name doesn't
matter—nor the place. Here you are, sitting on a block of
stock that hasn't been listed on the market all the years
you've owned it. Now comes a rap on your door—Paul's
there with another guy. He offers you, say, a dollar a share
for your junk. You know you can't raise a cent a share—
what do you do ? "

Slezak shifted out of the strip of sunlight. He watched
the Canadian's expression carefully. " If this stock's
unlisted and worthless, how do they know I've got it ? "

Russell smiled ironically. " That's a nice suspicious
touch that's in character. But keep it under control.
Figure it out," he urged. " You *know* this stock is worthless
—do you take Paul's offer ? If not, why ? "

Slezak decided, vaguely irritated by the Canadian's
superiority in expertise. " I sell."

" But reluctantly," Russell pointed out. " Remember
you're a wealthy man. You're not over-anxious to sell.
Your first reaction must be, if this stuff's worth a dollar
a throw to them, it's worth it to me ! Don't worry—Paul
will persuade you to sell. You'll agree to a sensible profit."

" Who's the guy *with* Sergeant ? " Slezak asked.

Russell was putting question and answer with patience.
" He's the mark—but the less you know about that the
better. Concentrate on your own part. Choose a name and
background you can use naturally. And for God's sake,

cut out the grandstanding. One false note will put the skids under us."

The shaft of sunlight had moved to Slezak's neck. He basked, his voice casual. "What sort of money would a man part with on a story like this?"

Russell shrugged. "If we get hold of the right man, you could pick up twenty thousand dollars for your end."

Slezak multiplied the sum by three. He wet his mouth cautiously. "There's just one thing, Russell. Why are we being so coy about the mark. Haven't you got one already?"

Russell sounded puzzled. "What's *that* supposed to mean?"

Slezak's hand was on the paper in his pocket. "Isn't that what my money was for—expenses to play him?"

Russell's hand stopped half-way between matchbox and cigarette. He completed the gesture before answering. "For crissakes say what you mean—I lost my crystal ball!"

Slezak pulled the message from his pocket. He read— "Lunch at the Crillon! Who's Arthur Wontner—your grandfather?" He was suddenly on his feet. Lucy and Sergeant were coming into the forecourt. "Don't leave the hotel this afternoon," warned Slezak. "I'll be back."

Russell shook his head. "You're out of your mind— isn't there anything you believe?"

"Let's say I like to be well-informed," answered Slezak. The cab he flagged down was behind Sergeant and the girl all the way to the Crillon.

CHAPTER VIII

THURSDAY P.M.

It was a long time before Russell moved from the shade of the tree. He scuffed through the longish grass uncertainly. Whatever Slezak intended there was no way of stopping him. Neither instinct nor logic was of any use in figuring the pilot's next move. A phone call to the Crillon would achieve nothing. If Slezak intended staging one of his confrontations, Paul would see him soon enough. If nothing more sinister was on his mind than one of his gumshoe acts, they'd hear about it later.

The beds in the room were still unmade. He waited a while for his connection with the villa at St. Cloud. They would need the best props that Doc Springer could provide. Stock certificates, letters-of-credit, cable forms, and the stamps for dating them. He gave Springer the order, weary of the other's inevitable sales-talk.

" Sure, Doc. I get the picture. You're letting us have top-grade paper and you want cash or a percentage. It'll be cash. I'll pick the stuff up some time to-day."

He checked his watch. It was a quarter past one. Slezak's last instructions had been definite. There was no sense in leaving the hotel. Russell made his way down to the restaurant. His meal finished, he sat hidden in a corner of the lounge. It was late afternoon when Sergeant returned. Russell watched the pair as far as the reception desk. A page took the wrapped box of flowers that Lucy was carrying. Both collected their room keys. Something the girl said made her father smile. Tucking her hand under his arm, he led her to the elevator.

Russell lowered the newspaper shielding him. Another cab was pulling into the forecourt. As Slezak passed the cigar stand, Russell called him.

The pilot whirled. In spite of his heaviness his reflexes were cat-fast. A wide grin spread on his face. He eased himself into a seat beside the Canadian.

Most of the tables in the lounge were occupied by French people, fussing over their afternoon tea. An elderly English couple sat a few yards away, rigidly disapproving.

Russell spoke quietly. " Whatever you're going to say, keep your voice down. We've got an audience." He pulled his chair behind a pillar as Lucy Sergeant came into sight.

He followed her till she disappeared through the door of the beauty parlour.

Slezak wagged his head. " You too ! Now I'd have thought something with a little more speed would be more your line. But there it is, you can never tell." He seemed highly pleased with himself.

Russell had the certainty that somewhere, sometime, he'd drive a fist into this smiling face. Measuring the long reach of Slezak's arms, he told himself that the first time could well be the last. His voice was steady. " You want to talk business or about my taste in women ? "

Slezak shot out one finger after another, making his points. " Arthur Wontner. Fifty-eight years old, an American citizen. President of Atlantic Fabric and Belting Corporation with plants in Ohio and Zürich, Switzerland."

Russell paid silent and reluctant tribute to Slezak's pertinacity. The guy had more cards up his sleeve than a children's conjuror. " What did you do ? " asked Russell. " Read his palm ? "

Slezak shook his heavy blond head. " I told you I had friends in the city. Who knows Arthur Wontner staying at the Crillon, I wondered. Turns out he's got an account with the airline. The office here seem to know a lot about him. Maybe not as much as you guys but enough to make me very interested." His look was bland.

Russell leaned forward. " I'd like to get something straight. The airline fired you—what makes everyone here so anxious to hold your hand ? "

" Not everyone," corrected Slezak. His eyes were half-closed. " Just one chick at Head Office. We've been very close."

The pilot's complacency gave Russell the clue he had been seeking. Behind Slezak's quick-witted cunning was a weakness that might be turned to use. The guy was just another great lover.

Slezak narrowed his eyes, reducing them to slits in puffy tissue. " I asked myself what would a con-man and his girl be doing with a man like Wontner—buying belting ? "

He smiled till the bridgework showed at the ends of his mouth. "You don't think I'm very bright," he reproved. "There's something else. Wontner's booked on a flight to Zürich to-morrow. Now I'll guess that was your next move!"

Russell shifted warily. Sergeant's association with his daughter was warping his sense of judgment. The pilot's news could be used to force Sergeant's hand. If Wontner was leaving town, there was no time to be lost. He came to his feet. "We'd better go upstairs."

Sergeant was lying on his bed, a towel across his face shielding his eyes from the light. He struggled up as they came into the room.

Russell shut the door carefully. "Things have been happening, Paul. It turns out our friend's not satisfied about Wontner. He thinks we're holding out. Either we play Wontner or it's trouble."

Sergeant swung his short legs to the floor, his face dismayed. "You're wrong, Slezak. Look—I never knew he existed till yesterday. He was on the plane with my daughter."

"Suppose we keep the daughter bit for people like Wontner," said Slezak dryly. "I want you to get to work on this guy before he gives you the slip."

"He's leaving for Zürich to-morrow, Paul." Russell was at the window. "Remember what I told you last night."

Sergeant found a half-smoked cigar—relit it. He stood for a while, rolling the acrid stub between his fingers. "I've got nothing to gain by lying. I've got trouble that even you wouldn't wish on me. But I don't want to touch this guy." He watched Slezak's reaction anxiously.

Russell shook his head. There was neither dignity nor use in the old man displaying his misery for Slezak's disbelief. The Canadian spoke hurriedly. "You're wasting your time, Pop. It's Wontner or Slezak blows the whistle."

The pilot was cautious—as if even now he sensed complicity. "You heard him," he said shortly.

Sergeant stubbed out his butt, looking from one to the

other. He made an obvious effort, his voice heavy with reluctance. " O.K. How do we know Wontner leaves to-morrow ? "

Slezak told him. The old man's mind worked quickly, whittling his plan free of deadwood. " He's never seen either of you, has he—whatever happens you've both got to keep out of his sight till I give you the word. I'll need props in a hurry, Gordy. We'll use Zürich for the pay-off —that means I'll have to start playing Wontner to-night."

" I already called Springer," said Russell. Once Sergeant had made his decision, all his partner's skill and determination would be at work. " The stuff'll be ready this afternoon. I said I'll collect it. Springer wants two bills."

Sergeant counted two hundred dollars from his wallet. " That's another reason for speed. The bankroll's getting light. Go over to Springer's right away. Send whatever I need back in a cab then see about your tickets. You can check out on the way down."

Russell was already throwing clothing into his bags. " How soon can *you* get out of your hotel ? " asked Sergeant.

Slezak sniffed cautiously at the question. " Ten minutes," he answered.

Russell zipped the last of his bags. " You're going to have to give Paul his passport back. And remember, we don't know him from a hole in the ground from now on till we meet in Zürich." He shrugged as the pilot showed hesitation. " I don't make the rules. They've been playing these rackets this way since before you were born."

Slezak tossed Sergeant's passport on the bed. " As long as *you're* with me, Russell ! You wouldn't want to see your boy in the lock-up, would you, old-timer ? "

Sergeant's voice was coloured with irritation. " You're being a little too smart. If this deal's to go through, you'll do what I say, Slezak, twenty-four hours a day. Is that understood ? "

The pilot threw his hand out in mock contrition. He made no attempt to hide his amusement as Russell spoke.

" What will you do about Lucy ? "

It was obvious that the prospect disturbed Sergeant. He looked doubtful. " I'll have to handle that my own way. But for the record, we're converting my securities. You've gone on to Zürich to make the first arrangements."

The Canadian picked up his bags. " Isn't that taking a chance ? What happens if we all run into one another in Zürich ? Why can't you leave her here ? "

Sergeant's refusal was positive. " In Paris—alone ? No —I'll take the responsibility, Gordy. There's no need for her to meet anyone. We'll just have to be doubly careful on that score."

Russell shrugged. " Whatever you say. I'll call you as soon as we get into Zürich. I'd better use the *Baur au Lac*. There's one other thing—Wontner knows your right name. What can we do about that ? "

" Nothing—I've got to take my chances." The old man considered them both thoughtfully. " We'd better fix names for you two. The hell with it—best keep them short and easy to remember. Gordon Redding and Stanley Sears. Time's getting short—you'd better be on your way." He pushed some more money at the Canadian.

Russell had the door open. His voice was uncertain. " I'll call to-night then, between eleven and twelve. If there's any trouble, you'll let me know ? "

" There'll be no trouble," said Sergeant steadily. " Not as long as you both use your heads."

The confident smile vanished as he shut the door behind them. He stood quietly at the window till he saw their cab drive away. Russell's hurried packing had left the room in disorder. Sergeant worked painstakingly, closing drawers, destroying useless bits of paper. When he was done, he slumped in the chair.

Over the years, he must have lived hundreds of scenes like this—the last few hours before staking your liberty against another man's money. If he'd ever had Gordy's subconscious reluctance to larceny, it was too long ago to remember. Repetition of risk had left him with a clear-cut attitude to conventional morality. Failure alone was reprehensible. Now he was suddenly old and success didn't seem to matter. Nothing mattered except Lucy's peace of mind. He made his plans with an unaccustomed sense of foreboding.

The girl at the switchboard took five minutes to locate Lucy under a hair-dryer. The old man forced assurance into his voice. "I thought you'd like to hear the news, honey. I've just seen Gordy off to Switzerland. He has my power-of-attorney to raise money. We'll follow to-morrow. Another few days and you can have the doctor make reservations for your mother at the clinic."

He put down the phone, shamed by her gratitude. One more call reached Wontner at the American Club. Sergeant's suggestion of drinks that evening was accepted. In spite of his relief he felt no enthusiasm at the prospect.

A knock on the door heralded a page with a brown paper parcel. Once alone, Sergeant cut the string impatiently and spread out the contents. It was a comprehensive outfit. A sheaf of cable blanks—three date stamps and an ink pad. Heavily embossed writing-paper and a sample of stock certificates—Russell would have the bulk of it. Paper and stock certificates bore the same title.

CANADA UNION MINING COMPANY

Sergeant held the certificates to the light. They were an example of high-class engraving on watermarked quality paper. Hundreds of companies like this existed—properly formed and registered. The promoters usually took a lease on some worked-out property near a well-known mine. The stock always finished in the hands of people like Doc Springer. Each certificate bore a face value of five hundred dollars. It was hardly worth the cost of the engraving.

He sat down at the typewriter he had borrowed from the management. Centering the sheet of Canada Union paper, he handled the machine competently. When he was done he read the letter through carefully.

CANADA UNION MINING COMPANY
Head Office
Bay Street
Toronto, Ont.
11th August, 1961

PRIVATE AND CONFIDENTIAL.

MY DEAR PAUL,

There are excellent reasons for the cautious note above. I rely completely on your discretion. I came up here a month ago with George Grant (Lever and Grant). We were engaged to run independent tests on Canada Union's Number One reef. Though the other reefs were played out years ago—*this one was never worked*.

The results of our tests were fantastic. Number One is producing high-grade ore extending in depth to the limits of the property. You'll understand that both George and I had to sign the usual undertakings of professional secrecy. (One reason why this letter must be kept completely confidential.) Any leakage of this news at this stage could ruin me.

The position is as follows. The Company has sealed off Number One reef completely and stopped all work on the property. A Toronto syndicate has been formed to buy up all stock in Canada Union. Most of this stock is held in Europe. One of the syndicate's agents is on his way to Zürich with instructions to buy up Swiss holdings at a reasonable price. (He's gone up to $55 a share in London!) *One of the principal stockholders is living near Zürich!* So far the syndicate has been unable to find his address in what company registers are left here. I HAVE FOUND IT! He is Stanley Sears, c/o Privatbank, Bahnhofstrasse, Zürich.

Now this is what you do. Get hold of this guy at once. Take out a short-term option on all his stock (he holds nearly three-quarters of a million dollars at par). There is no possible way in which our report can have reached Sears. You should be able to buy at well under five bucks, reselling immediately to the syndicate's agent at fifty. If you stick out for fifty, he'll pay. Those are his instructions. The agent's name is Gordon Redding. Reservations have been made for him at the *Baur au Lac Hotel* in Zürich.

I suggest that we split profits on an even basis. You're in the business, Paul. I don't have to tell you to steer clear of brokers and bankers. The least hint of what you're up to and the vultures will come flying!

This is a chance to make a considerable fortune so go to it. Keep in touch with me by cable but NOT to the above address. Use Margery's house for any communications.

Best and for crissakes lose no time!

Sergeant made the signature bold and indecipherable.

Folding the letter carefully he inserted it in an envelope addressed to himself at the hotel. Next he gummed Canadian airmail postage on the corner. Last came the cancellation stamp. Sergeant inspected the result narrowly. Everything was perfect. Date—time of mailing—even the imprint of the Toronto sub-post office. Using a knife he slit open the envelope and put it in an inside pocket.

Back on his bed, he put the towel over his eyes again and slept. It was six-thirty when the buzzing phone awakened him.

He dressed slowly, choosing dark suit, tie and shoes. The final effect was one of grave respectability. The outward and visible sign of an inward and spiritual grace, he thought wryly. A noise drew his attention. A telegram had been pushed under the door. He tore the thin paper hurriedly. The message had been sent an hour ago from the *aérogare* on the Quai d'Orsay.

ARRIVE ZÜRICH SEVENTEEN HOURS STOP ALL CONTROLLED
GORDY

Sergeant flushed the telegram down the lavatory bowl. Once committed, he made even the minor aspects of self-preservation automatically.

He relaxed in a chair, assimilating the implications of his position. Slezak's arrival and subsequent antics were beyond his experience. In nearly forty years in the game, he'd never heard of a similar case. The pattern of a sucker's behaviour was standard once he was beaten. Either he went to the police or vanity shut his mouth. Occasionally there was some freak compromise. A victim thought to have returned home thousands of miles away stayed on. You turned a corner on the street and there he was—the guy you'd robbed the month before. Many years before, it had happened to Sergeant. He walked into a Knightsbridge store and came face to face with an irate horse-breeder from Virginia. The man had one idea—to get his money back without either police or publicity. This much was certain—Slezak must be dropped peaceably and quickly. For the moment, Gordy's hostility to the man was under control. But the Canadian's impulsion into occasional violence could be a danger. Slezak needed the stiletto, not the bludgeon. The verdict left no disquiet in the old man's mind. He made one last self-appraisal in the long mirror. The white hair was brushed smooth, the chubby face serene. He shut the bedroom door on all thought of the pilot.

Lucy was waiting in the lounge. She wore the same dress as the night before. Neither her time nor her money had been wasted in the beauty parlour, he thought. She came across to meet him, poised and confident. For a moment she held him at arm's length. " You're gorgeous—positively gorgeous ! " She decided. She gave his tie a little tug. " Do you know what I've been thinking this afternoon ? " He shook his head, content in this newfound intimacy. She found the crook of his elbow, steering him towards the bar. As they walked he realised how tall she was, the spike heels of her shoes putting her a head above him.

" I've been thinking how lucky I am ! " She leaned both elbows on the counter, watching his expression in the glass. " I've got a feeling I know what you're going to do," she said suddenly.

He speared a tiny onion, amazed at the steadiness of his

fingers. He met her smile, having to clear his voice before it could be trusted. " What am I going to do ? "

She touched the back of her neck, her face rueful. " You're going to stand me up for another woman—and to think I just wasted ten dollars ! "

The heart of vodka in his drink steadied him. The barman had moved away, his sallow face blank with professional discretion. Heavy glass doors shut out the babble from the lounge, making the long dim room a refuge from reality. He turned to face her. " I've got to go out for an hour on business, darling. Believe me, I'd sooner stay here with you."

Her voice was disbelieving but she still smiled affectionately. " Men ! I expect you're the ringleader—not Gordy." She lifted her glass, making a face at the sharpness of the lime.

He tried to maintain the lightness of her tone. " I may be an hour—possibly more. If I'm not back by eight-thirty, better start your meal alone." He watched her from the corner of his eye. Twenty-four hours before, she'd been on edge—now she was relaxed and radiant. The implication was frightening. She was relying on him completely. He spoke to her diffidently—uncertain how to phrase his question. " You're a good-looking girl, Lucy. Hasn't there been anyone special back in California ? "

She pushed her hand in the cuff of his sleeve, giving his wrist a small tug. " No one special. You'd better go—ladies don't like to be kept waiting. It doesn't matter if you're not back. There are letters I must write if we're leaving for Switzerland to-morrow."

He lowered short legs to the ground, standing in front of her. " Suppose I retired, Lucy . . ." He shook his head, defeated by the futility of the thought. " Ah hell, your place is with your mother."

She touched his cheek briefly with her lips, indifferent to the barman. " Good night, Daddy. If you ever buy a shack by the river, keep a bunk for me."

The air outside was warm and fresh with the smell of

the Bois. He walked slowly towards the blaze of lights marking the crest of the Champs-Élysées. On down the glittering slope, passing the crowded cafés, the theatre queues. Beyond the six-lane traffic a sign winked high on the façade of a department store. Twenty-five—no, thirty years ago—there'd been a hotel there. A room on the top floor, stuffy with the smell of camphor and oranges. On the wide gilt-framed bed, Lucy's mother, peeling the fruit as she kicked her shoes at the wall. They had stood on the tiny balcony in the early hours of the morning, watching the scene below. It all seemed a very long time ago. And perhaps rightly so. Paris was for the young and its memories best forgotten.

At the end of the Rue Lincoln, he turned into a Spanish-styled patio. Old sherry casks made the tables. Soft guitar music came from behind wrought-iron and foliage.

He peered uncertainly about him. Wontner stood up in the shadows. He wore evening clothes, a cummerbund circling his soft pleated shirt. He collected a chair for Sergeant. Candlelight touched the strong line of his jaw. His voice was courteous. " I'm sorry to drag you over here —I'm meeting some people for dinner later. There's an amontillado that I can recommend."

The nutty wine was bland after the bite of the vodka. Sergeant savoured its taste and started his pitch. His face was troubled.

" You may find what I'm going to say extraordinary. A man of my age doesn't usually seek advice on ethics from a comparative stranger."

Wontner smiled. " I wouldn't have thought it much use. What people call ethics seem to me to be so personal that exterior advice becomes invidious. It's nothing to do with Lucy, is it ? " His voice was sharp with concern.

Sergeant shook his head. " No—not really. The truth is that I'm looking for approval for a decision I've already taken." He weighed the prepared letter in his hand. " We're both men of the world. Before I give you this letter I'd like to be certain that you'll respect its confidence."

The ominous significance of the last word hung till it was finally lost in the sound of the guitar. The other man's face was a blur in the half-light.

Wontner stretched out a hand. He donned spectacles and read the letter with care. When he was done, he folded it precisely and returned it to Sergeant. The spectacle case snapped shut and he shrugged his shoulders. His voice held neither undue interest nor suspicion. " What's your problem ? "

Sergeant was making patterns with the bottom of his glass. " This boy's the son of a very old friend—a mining engineer who's done work for my companies. It's possible that the issue is personal rather than ethical. If I take advantage of this information, I'm fostering the lad's deliberate betrayal of his professional code. If I refuse, I lose a great deal of money."

Wontner sat in silence. Then his chair scraped back. " How about this syndicate ? Hasn't it occurred to you that they're defrauding every single stockholder in the company ? It's one of those clear-cut cases impossible to prove in a court of law. There's no Boy Scout Code on Wall Street, Sergeant—you know that as well as I do. This boy's behaviour is something else. He appears to have made his own decision. I don't know that anything you might do would alter it."

Sergeant's head was bent. " What you're saying is that if it wasn't me it would be someone else ? "

" Precisely," answered Wontner. " You know, big business is about as moral as war. The way the world's run, both seem necessary. You're a man of sensibilities, Sergeant. Take my advice and keep them for your daughter."

Sergeant nodded slowly. " I guess you're right. I ought to apologise for wishing all this on you. A man needs someone who talks his own language—that'll have to be my excuse."

" Forget it—where's Lucy to-night ? "

" Writing letters," answered Sergeant. " She's a conscientious girl—I hope life's kind to her."

"It will be." Wontner looked at his watch. "You'll have to excuse me now, I've got these people arriving any minute." He stood up, holding on to the back of his chair. His expression was plain in the light from a wall bracket. He was smiling. "Are you going to Zürich?"

Sergeant came to his feet. "I guess so. And if I'm in trouble with my conscience I'll remember all you said."

Wontner put out a hand. His grip was firm and friendly. "Then we'll probably see one another. I'm leaving for Switzerland to-morrow, myself. I have an office in Zürich. Give me a ring there. The number is 76–789. My father used to say something that seems to cover your problem, Sergeant—'Conscience is the still small voice of someone else!' Good night and my love to Lucy!"

CHAPTER IX

FRIDAY A.M.

ALL NIGHT, thunder had rolled through the mountain tops. Giant drums heralding sheet-lightning over the lake beyond Russell's window. For hours he had watched sleepless, listening to Slezak's heavy breathing. Each vivid flash lit the room brilliantly. The man in the other bed lay with his face half-buried in the pillow. It was early morning before Russell lost consciousness.

The last patches of wet on the Bahnhofstrasse were drying in the sun as he left the hotel. Zürich was already establishing her pattern of order, cleanliness and prosperity. Ultra-modern store fronts exposed cameras, books, impressionist paintings, automobiles. Scent, cashmere overcoats and Salvadorean coffee. The sober Zürich burgher required the best the world had to offer—the great stone-built banks were a symbol of his ability to pay for it.

Past the square with its street-car junction, Russell turned into Barengasse. The address the porter had given him was a hundred yards in the direction of the river. He climbed granite steps to the air-conditioned office. It was half-past eight and he had left Slezak sleeping.

The young clerk was a model of Swiss business efficiency. Neatly dressed, at ease in four languages and keen. His English was formal—his accent heavy.

"Mr. Redding? They telephoned from the hotel to say you are coming." He led the way to a small ante-room. The outside wall was a sheet of glass high above the cabin-cruisers moored in the river. The clerk waited till Russell was seated. "Please—how may we help you?"

Russell spoke slowly, giving the clerk time to assimilate the importance of the announcement. "I'm secretary to Mr. Stanley Sears. Mr. Sears's name will be familiar to you, naturally?"

The clerk was well-trained. He steered expertly between truth and falsehood. "I am not quite certain—but I believe I have heard this name." His smile indicated a possible lack of sophistication.

"Mr. Sears *is* Tidal Oil," Russell said shortly. "He needs a furnished house. Your name was given as being the best people in the city."

The clerk was politely incredulous. "A furnished house in Zürich! These things hardly exist, Mr. Redding. Our customs are different to yours. Chalets for summer or winter sports. New and old apartments without furniture—this is our business. What sort of house would you require?"

Russell gave the matter his attention. "Well—to start with I'd better tell you that Mr. Sears suffers from insomnia. There'd have to be at least four bedrooms. Separate quarters for the staff. Space and seclusion. That's the note to aim at. Money's of less importance to Mr. Sears than comfort. We'd like some land attached to the property —preferably wooded."

The clerk looked up quickly. "Then not in the city! So it is just possible." He pressed a buzzer and gave the girl who answered an instruction. She returned with a file and sheaf of photographs. The young man handled them with respect. " This house is twenty kilometres from the city. On the lake in a village called Freienbach." He read the particulars from the file. " Ten hectares of garden, a private landing-stage with a cabin-cruiser. The garage and servants' rooms are separate. This house is modern and very luxurious." He found the word with satisfaction and pushed the pile of glossy prints across the table.

Russell studied them. The low timber-built house was built in contemporary Swedish style. A spruce or larch thicket screened the buildings from the highway. On the shore side was a boat-house and tennis court. " It's summer-time—what about the noise ? " He had to create a definite picture of a man both rich and irascible.

The clerk was emphatic. " This is one half-kilometre away from the routes of the lake steamers. From strangers you are protected by. . . ."—he pinned the print with his index finger—" poles in the water ? " he hazarded.

" Piles," said Russell.

The clerk shrugged, stacking the photographs. " Nothing comes near—only swans. This is the house of Doctor Thaler. He is in China. We would not be able to give the house for less than one year. The rent—" he sought the figure happily—" the rent is two thousand Swiss francs each month. Doctor Thaler would require references."

Russell made a calculation in his mind. The rent was about five hundred dollars a month. " I don't think either the length or the terms of the lease will bother Mr. Sears if the house is what he wants." He kept his tone casual, inviting understanding of a quixotic employer. " Speed is the most essential thing. To-day or to-morrow would be the latest for the lease to be signed. Mr. Sears has made this plain."

The young man added a couple of curlicues to the entry against Russell's name. " This is difficult. I cannot give an answer. You will have to see my director. Doctor Thaler's house has many beautiful things, Mr. Redding. References are necessary for our client's protection." He spread his hands, amiable yet cautious.

Russell nodded. " That's normal enough. I'm prepared to give you a cheque for a year in advance. You could take up this reference by telephone. The others by mail." He twisted the paper so that the man could read what he had written. " Doctor Geronimo Springer. St. Cloud 1–7486. Doctor Springer is our ex-ambassador to Brazil and a personal friend of Mr. Sears." The statement had just the right touch of grandiloquence.

It appeared to have effect. The clerk gathered his documents. " If you will excuse me ? " He closed the door to the office leaving Russell alone. The Canadian stood at the window. A coxed four was pulling into the centre of the stream, the voice of the small humped figure calling the stroke clear in the thin air. Far beyond the launches and pleasure steamers would be Freienbach. This house was perfect. Once they were in the place the rest didn't matter. The names he would give as references would be genuine and of international standing. Only by the time they had been checked, he and Sergeant would be a thousand miles away.

He turned confidently as the door opened. The clerk was carrying a bunch of keys. " The director will telephone Doctor Springer. If we go to the house, they will have an answer when we return. It is not for me to decide, but I think all things will be in order."

Outside, a Buick convertible was parked in a space where its licence number was painted on the ground. The young man opened the door. Russell climbed in beside him. The clerk eased the car to the narrow street. His hands seemed familiar with the controls.

" This is your car ? " Russell asked idly.

The young man smiled. He pressed a button, folding the top of the convertible back in its cavity. " The director is my uncle. It is his car."

Leaving the bridge on their left, they took the lake highway out of the city. The last suburb straggled into the valley to the west. Already the small bathing beaches were covered with sunburned bodies. Across the lake, the distant shoreline was hazy in the sun. A few sailing-boats tacked gracefully into the breeze. They drove through Thalwil and Richterswil, past the hotels and road-houses hugging the edge of the water. The Buick made good time on the deserted stretches of highway. Half a kilometre out of the tiny village of Freienbach, the driver pulled the car to the lake side of the highway. A white five-barred gate was set in a tall stone wall. Beyond it, a gravelled avenue curved through a belt of trees. The man gave the keys to Russell, smiling courteously.

"Will you unlock, please—the gate. This is the house."

The villa faced south. Behind it, a cropped lawn sloped to the lake shore. On the left, a tightly-hedged pathway led to a two-storied brick garage. The clerk found the key to the front door. The interior was in complete darkness. He used a switch. Electrically-controlled shutters rolled into the thickness of the timber, letting in daylight.

Walls, doors and ceilings were pastel shaded. The paintings, glass and furniture had been chosen for form and colour rather than period. Russell followed the young Swiss through bright, comfortable rooms. The clerk's commentary was unnecessary. The owner's taste was evident. Money had neither been spared nor wasted. Beds and carpets were deep and soft. The bathrooms and kitchen a mixture of gadgets and tiled brilliance. Not a sitting- or bedroom was without its shelved books.

They walked down the path to the garage. A key in a switch operated the weighted steel door vertically. The second story consisted of kitchen, bathroom and living quarters. The boat-house jutted forty feet into the lake. Inside, a cabin-cruiser hooded in canvas, slapped in green water. Above it, a dinghy and canoe were hoisted on slings. The creak of timber only accentuated the impression of isolation.

The Swiss turned the key in the boat-house. " Do you think this will be suitable ? "

Russell matched his stride to the other's as they made their way back to the car. " It's small, but it'll do ! "

They reached the city centre before ten had struck. The principal of the firm was a small bearded man with a high, starched collar. He greeted Russell courteously, " I have just talked with Doctor Springer on the telephone. He will confirm our conversation in writing. You will understand that we need a further reference ! "

Russell took a seat. " I'd like to have a word with you alone." When the young man had left the room, Russell spoke with deliberate emphasis. " I want you to understand my position clearly. I'm afraid Mr. Sears is accustomed to making conditions rather than accepting them. I left the hotel this morning with very definite instructions. Unless I go back with a signed lease—or at least authority to move into the house at once, we're wasting our time."

The director explored his beard with his fingers. " For two months there is nobody living in this house," he objected mildly. " Much is necessary first—cleaning and sweeping."

" It looked satisfactory to me," answered Russell. " We've got a man and his wife arriving from Paris to-day. They'll take care of all that." Sensing that the other was wavering he produced the cheque-book that had come in Springer's box of tricks. " I am authorised to pay a year's rent in advance. If you're not able to give me a decision now, I'm sorry. I'll have to try somewhere else."

The prospect seemed to move the bearded man to action. He calculated on paper, giving Russell the sum in dollars. " I shall sign the lease, Mr. Redding. You will leave me the name of another reference, please. A caretaker comes twice a week. He cuts grass and attends the garden. His wages are paid by Doctor Thaler."

Russell completed the cheque. The account with the Royal Reserve Bank of Canada was non-existent. But it would serve its purpose before the fraud was established.

He collected lease, receipt and keys and returned to the hotel. Slezak was having breakfast on the terrace, his big body lazy in the sun. He lifted a hand. His eyes were blank behind tinted spectacles.

96

" Jesus God! The ball of fire himself! What's the matter—is your bed uncomfortable or something ! "

" If you want short hours, try another racket ! " Russell said curtly. " We're taking a drive—your house is ready ! "

They carried Slezak's bags to the rented Volkswagen parked in front of the hotel and drove back to Freienbach. Beyond the white gate, the grounds were quiet under a hot sun. Russell rolled back the shutters, opening windows on to the heavy scent of massed wallflowers. Slezak wandered through the house, hefting cut glass, studying the formless splash of colour of a painting with irony. Finding a zinc-lined drinks cupboard, he regarded the well-stocked racks with satisfaction. He poured himself a half-tumbler of whisky and soda. Through the picture window, a few swans sailed contentedly between the piles protecting the foreshore. Slezak nodded approval.

" Very nice indeed ! All we need now is a couple of chicks ! " He swung round, the broad smile back on his face. " Listen, Russell—I've got an idea. What do you say we pick up a couple of chicks ? I've never known a hotel porter without an address book. There's nothing we can do till to-morrow. There's a lot of drinking time till then."

The Canadian closed the cupboard door with his knee. His voice was savagely quiet. " You get this straight, Slezak. Right now an old man is taking a chance for all of us. You're a thief now—we use a set of rules for our self-protection. There'll be no drinking and no chicks." He almost spat the last word.

Slezak's mouth twisted. His eyes were half-shut. " Get out of the pulpit," he said easily. " You probably get yours with the blonde anyway ! "

Russell's nails dug deep in his palms. He kept his voice steady with an effort. " There'll be no drinking and no women," he repeated. " That goes for both of us."

Slezak shrugged, apparently content to accept defeat. " What are you getting so hot about ? Suppose you tell me what I'm supposed to do in this dump—wait till Sergeant bangs on the door with a pocketful of money ? "

"We'll drive into the village for food," answered Russell. "You've got a phone—if you're in doubt, call me at the hotel. There can't be one false note. No stale butts or dirty glasses. This room's got to look as it does now. Impeccable!"

Slezak opened the cupboard door again, making each move with deliberation. His voice was sarcastic. "Two people arrive here to-morrow. I open the door myself. Who's supposed to do the housework—the pixies?"

Russell was patient. "You're an edgy, neurotic character. You keep your staff where they belong—over the garage. Especially when you have visitors. Is that clear?"

Slezak carried his bags to the bedroom door. He came back, kneading the knuckles of his right hand. "You bother me, Russell," he said quietly. "And I don't like it. Now let's get that grub!"

When they had shopped in the village for groceries, Russell made fast time back to the city. Sergeant was a rapid operator. Things could break at any moment.

In the hotel room, the Canadian set the scene. First came the gold, black and white stock certificates. He counted off fifty. The rest of them were for Slezak. These Russell sealed in a large envelope bearing the imprint of a well-known bank. The loose fifty had to go to Sergeant's hotel. Paul had sounded full of confidence the night before. He and Lucy were taking the eight o'clock *rapide* from Paris. They'd be in Zürich in the afternoon. All Sergeant knew was that Wontner had already left for Switzerland.

Russell added a few more documents to Slezak's pile— creating an imposing portfolio that a man might well have lodged at his bank. The whole was tied with banking tape and heavily sealed with wax. His own props were simpler. Cheque-book and brief-case. With any sort of luck, Wontner would be in this room before the day was out—preferably alone.

Russell packed away the unused paraphernalia, locking the suitcase. He sat down, dragging his chair to face the window. His hand hid the nervous twitch in his lip. It was impossible for him to shut out thoughts of Lucy. His first unreasoned enmity for her was gone. He was now involved in her difficulties. Wasn't that enough . . . the thought of any deeper emotional entanglement was ridiculous. A few more days, weeks—and she'd be back where she came from. Leaving them both with a smile and a curtsy. The prospect was vaguely unpleasant. He'd been too long away from the type, he told himself. And this was Paul's daughter.

CHAPTER X

FRIDAY P.M.

ONCE OUT of the railroad station, the cab turned left over the bridge. It climbed past the new university buildings, taking the winding road that led to the zoo. Sergeant was sitting so that pressure on his haunch spared the rheumatic pain. He kept his eyes on the passing scene to get relief from the girl's shrewd questioning. The trip from Paris had not been easy on his peace of mind. Lucy's manner had changed overnight. The buoyancy was still there, together with a new possessiveness that should have flattered him. Bullying her way to a corner seat on the train, she had insisted that he occupied it. It had been the same in the dining-car. He ate a meal that she chose, solicitous of his digestion. The determined interest behind it all worried him. Everything was of interest to her. The way he and Gordy lived on their travels—the likes and needs of two men without feminine care. He'd dropped Wontner's name casually—hinting at a probable meeting in Zürich. Her only apparent reactions were surprise and pleasure. One thing was plain—as soon as this was all over, he had to get the three of them out of town in a hurry. Stockholm would make an unlikely bolt-hole. Lucy could take the Polar route home. He and Gordy would head south again with whatever money was left.

Thought of the future disturbed him. The only alternative to theft was the classic refuge of a rogue whose nerve has gone. He pictured himself the owner of some sleazy hang-out for con-men. Despised and mistrusted by thieves and their catchers alike. There had to be another answer.

He felt the tug at his sleeve. Lucy was smiling.

" What about him ? " she asked.

He stared stupidly. " What about who, honey ? "

She shook her head. " You're day-dreaming. You distinctly said ' Gordy ' then grunted." She used her lipstick. The indifference of her next question was a little overdone. " Where *is* Mr. Russell ? I imagined he'd be at the station."

The cab climbed a narrower road free of street-car tracks. Now came solid houses set in tree-lined gardens. Sergeant's voice was sugary with assurance.

" I doubt if you'll see Gordy for a few days. If you do, I'll want to know why. He's supposed to be too busy for social activities."

Her head was averted. " Why hasn't he married—don't you pay him enough money ? "

Sergeant answered impulsively. " Maybe he knows when he's well-off."

Eyes troubled behind swinging hair, she considered him. " Do you really hate women as much as all that ? " she asked quietly.

He eased the rheumatic ache in his flank and smiled. " Not really. You make them worth while."

The old-fashioned hotel perched on top of the hill. It was a rambling building shut out from the sun by gloomy evergreens. Sergeant's room was at the front—big, comfortable and smelling of floor polish. He unpacked and poured himself a shot from the bottle wrapped in his pyjamas. He was glad Russell was not there to see him break his own cardinal rule. But he needed a drink. Donning spectacles, he searched the leather-bound telephone directory. The address he was looking for was there. ATLANTIC FABRIC

AND BELTING CORPORATION, with a number on Bleicherweg. He picked up the phone. The girl's voice was briskly American.

" Mr. Wontner ? I'm afraid he's in conference, Mr. Sergeant. Can I get him to ring you back ? "

" If you please." Lighting a cigar, he sat with the instrument across his knees. The next few minutes would tell whether or not Wontner was hooked. It seemed a long time before the phone came to life. He forced himself to sound relaxed.

" Arthur ! Sure—a very good trip ! She's fine—sends her love. Look—something came up since I saw you last night. Would it be possible for us to meet ? Yes—I'd prefer it as soon as you can make it."

He held his breath, standing on the edge of a precipice. The sound of rushing water was clear. Wontner's answer pulled him back to reality.

" I could do that, yes, Paul. You'd better come down to my office. I'll be waiting for you. It's the Stock Exchange Building, any cab-driver will know it ! "

Sergeant carried the phone to the table, his face thoughtful. He peered into the mirror, brushing the thick white hair smooth above his ears. The Stock Exchange Building. Had Wontner smiled as he said it—the smile of a man content to bide his time !

Sergeant found the envelope Russell had sent over and ordered a cab.

The Stock Exchange Building angled the corner of Bleicherweg. The whole of the fifth floor was occupied by the offices of Atlantic Fabric and Belting Corporation. A ground-glass panel was marked INQUIRIES. Sergeant pushed it open. He followed the girl to a well-lighted room. Wontner was waiting for him. On the far wall, a picture showed a snowbound chalet—a group of children posed with a Saint Bernard dog. Behind the desk was a framed diploma from the Harvard School of Business. Wontner's silk jacket was thrown across a chair. He removed it to make room for Sergeant and pushed aside a pile of letters.

" I get a cramp in the arm every time I come here ! This is Landholt's office—our Swiss director." He leaned back easily in his chair, capping and recapping the blunt pen between his fingers.

Sergeant settled himself awkwardly. His hip troubled him. It was nearly five years since anyone had treated it. He took his time lighting the thin panatella. Seconds now and there'd be no turning back. The pitch would be either accepted or rejected. But Wontner ought to be showing some sort of curiosity instead of fiddling with that goddam pen.

There was nothing Sergeant liked about this set-up. He was working under pressure—his real identity exposed and robbing a man with a claim on his gratitude. He threw the match in the ash-tray, forcing himself to go on. Thieves had no right to sentimental scruples.

" It's this business with Canada Mining Union. I got a package in Paris last night. The boy shipped it airmail express. He's managed to pick up seventy-two shares in Toronto. How or where, I don't know." He fished the envelope out and slid it across the desk. " Take a look," he invited.

Wontner's weight came down heavily, the front legs of his chair digging into the carpet. He held the envelope in his hand making no attempt to open it. " I checked this stock this afternoon. You couldn't get a market quote on a truck load," he said quietly.

The old man relaxed. Wontner was hooked. Sergeant hid his satisfaction with a show of anger. " Checked it. You had no right to do that ! All I told you about this affair was in confidence. . . ."

" Now hold your horses ! " Wontner lifted the envelope, emphasising his words. " It was a purely theoretical question put to a broker in the building. His answer was definite. There isn't any market for Canada Union. You can neither buy nor sell—I thought you'd be interested."

Sergeant blew a cloud of smoke. " If there is a quote at the end of to-day's trading I'll know who to thank for it.

A man in your position must know what a leak like this could do ! "

Wontner was nonplussed. He smiled apologetically. " It was the sort of thing a broker hears fifty times a day and forgets immediately. I saw the guy's reaction, Paul. Canada Union meant nothing to him—nothing at all ! "

Sergeant set his plump cheeks. " It was a crazy thing to do," he said stubbornly. Things were going better than he could have hoped for. Wontner certainly wasn't beyond the implications of a rigged market operation.

Wontner rubbed his bald head ruefully. " Well, maybe. It was meant to be a friendly gesture."

Sergeant nodded. " You couldn't have given me better news. All I hope is your friend's opinion of Canada Union stays unchanged for another week—open that envelope ! "

Wontner broke the seal, his brown eyes curious.

Sergeant hitched his chair closer to the desk. His voice was confidential. He had the certainty of the experienced billiard-player who watches the final pocket, indifferent to the ball's career from cushion to cushion.

" Things are happening fast," he said. " The syndicate's man is here in Zürich."

Wontner's mouth pursed slightly. He listened intently to every word.

" And I've got the address of the majority stockholder," Sergeant added quietly. " He's living twenty miles from the city."

The crisp sheaf of certificates rustled under Wontner's inspection. He held one to the light, exploring its texture as if able to determine its value by feel alone. He replaced the documents reluctantly in their cover.

" You're going to try these out on the agent—is that the scheme ? "

Sergeant nodded. " That's the scheme. I'm sorry if I jumped down your throat. Ever since this thing broke, I haven't been myself. One minute I think I'm wasting my time. The next, I'm dead certain of making a great

deal of money. This is going to tell me which is right!"
He made a gesture towards the envelope.

Wontner's voice was casual. "I see your point—what
I don't follow is how I fit into all this."

Sergeant's look was level. "This man Redding—the
agent. I wouldn't know him from a hole in the ground.
But he'll know me—at least by repute. If I take him the
stock personally, I run the risk of blowing the whole deal
skyhigh. Once the syndicate hears Paul Sergeant is interested, it's good night." He leaned forward, emphasising
his words. "You're the only man in Zürich I can
trust."

Wontner's voice was controlled. "I see. It doesn't
seem much of a proposition from my point of view. Look
at the facts—you unload a thing like this on me, saying you
trust me. I'm delighted you do it—nevertheless I can't
say I'm sold on the idea of acting as honorary broker.
Don't get me wrong, Paul. I mean no offence. I met you
—I like you. But suppose this deal goes sour—you'll
blame me!"

"Nobody will be to blame," Sergeant said quickly.
"Either Redding buys or he doesn't. If you prefer this
operation to be on a business footing, we'll do it that way.
What would you say was fair—remember, you risk nothing.
One per cent of the profits?"

Wontner draped his jacket round his shoulders. "That's
more than fair but I want no part of it. I'll tell you—the
whole scheme intrigues me—I'll do what you want for the
hell of it. One thing occurs to me. How will this Redding
react to a complete stranger walking in on him. Won't that
look suspicious?"

"You won't be a complete stranger," answered Sergeant.
"Say you're acting for Stanley Sears. Sears is the man
Redding's looking for."

Wontner spoke into the intercom, his eyes never leaving
Sergeant's face. "Get me Mr. Redding at the Baur-au-Lac
Hotel, please." The call came through immediately.
The conversation was brief. Wontner cradled the phone,

his expression impassive. "He'll see me right away. Will you wait?"

"I'll wait," answered Sergeant.

It was a half-hour before Wontner was back. He shut the door carefully behind him. He seemed determined to extract drama from the situation. He stood, one hand in his pocket, looking down at the old man.

"Don't play *that* young fellow cheap," he said thoughtfully. "You get your money all right, but whoever told you fifty-five dollars was wrong. Redding's best offer was fifty and he meant it." He put the cheque on the desk in front of Sergeant.

Sergeant turned over the slip of paper. The draft was for thirty-six hundred dollars and drawn on the Royal Reserve Bank of Canada. Gordy's signature was impressive.

Wontner was smiling. "I didn't bother asking him to have it certified. My hunch is that the money will be there. I had to sign the transfer slips in Sears's name." He was curiously intent. "Well, come on, say something! What's worrying you—the fifty dollars?"

Sergeant shook his head. He folded the cheque and put it into his wallet. "It's not the moment to say too much, Arthur. But you can be sure of one thing—I won't forget this."

Wontner presented his back to Sergeant. He groped in a cigarette box. "A deal like this takes a great deal of money to swing—cash money."

Sergeant watched him carefully. It was a matter of time now. "It'll take less than you imagine. I'm going to pick up short-term options on this stock. All I have to find is ten per cent. I'll use the syndicate's money to complete purchase."

Wontner swung round. "Why don't we have dinner together. Bring Lucy. I've got to drive out to the plant now, but I'll be back by seven."

Sergeant struggled up, complaining. "This goddam rheumatism's killing me. Fine, Arthur—but this is on me. We'll pick you up at your place at a quarter to eight."

The gloomy hotel had the advantage of numerous entrances. Sergeant used the window-door from garden to library. He stood for a moment, leafing the magazines on a circular table. Nobody else was in the room. He picked up a phone and asked for Russell's number. He spoke gradually, an eye on the glass partition leading to the hall.

" Gordy ! How did he go ? "

Russell's answer was almost contemptuous. " Like a log of wood. He came into the room like a clergyman at a county fair. There was one moment when I thought he was going to look under the bed. Listen, Paul—this guy's cagey. He was pumping me for names on the syndicate."

The old man's voice changed with sudden asperity. " Will you get off this line, Operator. I can't hear properly! " He waited for the tell-tale click but nothing happened. He resumed his normal voice.

" Don't worry about it, son. He can't wait to get in on the act. About Slezak—are you sure he won't play the clown, Gordy ? He mustn't move a yard from the house till we go there—is this clear ? "

Russell's voice was curt. " It's clear. He'll do as he's told. Listen—Paul, I've got this house under control for four days at the most. After that those references could bounce back at us by any mail."

Anxiety corrugated the old man's forehead. The pattern was familiar. The moment the action died on Gordy, his doubt started up. Sergeant answered with confidence. " We won't need anything *like* four days. Wontner's bound to have bank accounts here. We won't even have to wait for a cabled transfer of funds. Keep cracking the whip at Slezak. He's the weak link."

The Canadian's voice was hesitant. " You don't want me to tail Wontner ? "

Had any of this been played to the rules, the suggestion would have been valid. A fourth man would have lived in Wontner's pocket—reporting each move. The people he saw—the visits he made. But nothing here was classic—not even the reason for stealing Wontner's money.

" There's no need, Gordy," Sergeant said finally. " This guy's not going near the coppers. You concentrate on Slezak ! "

He made his way up the staircase. The drag at his hip was preferable to a possible encounter with the bunch of women waiting by the elevator. A coach had unloaded, its occupants milling across the hall. Sheep in poplin raincoats, he thought. They wore their cameras like bells and followed their guide with faithful uncomplaining eyes.

He tapped on Lucy's door. She was sitting at the desk, a writing-pad and teapot in front of her. He filled the empty cup and sat down gingerly on the bed. It was almost over, he thought wearily. A few days and she'd be gone. This could well be the last time they ever met. He imagined the small town she called home. Up on the heights, there'd be wide, shady streets where the taxpayers lived. Down below, a cluster of supermarket, gas-station and square white stores straggling to the edge of the Pacific. The only escapes from reality a couple of clapboard churches, a movie theatre and Rooney's Bar and Grill. Yet what could he offer her that was better. . . .

He put the lukewarm brew down untasted. " We're seeing Wontner for dinner, honey. I thought you'd be pleased."

Her quick self-appraisal added to his melancholy. She still reacted to an occasion with unspoiled enthusiasm.

" You'll have plenty of time," he added. He tucked a hundred-dollar bill into her hand. " I've bought you nothing yet. I want you to go out and get yourself the prettiest dress you can find."

She stood in front of the mirror, hitching the cotton frock as far as slim tanned knees. She pirouetted slowly, imitating a model's pivot. " You're an angel," she said happily. " I'll get something really snazzy. Something that will knock even the sophisticated Mr. Russell's eye out ! "

" Gordy won't be there," he said casually. " I told you —he's busy. Don't expect a gay evening—Wontner and

I will probably talk business. Maybe he dances—we'll see."

Her voice was curious. " Are you doing business with Mr. Wontner, Daddy ? "

As he searched for the right answer, she leaned across suddenly, cobalt eyes questioning.

" You haven't told him anything—not about Mother, have you ? " she demanded.

He shook his head. " Would I do a thing like that ! " He held her for a second in short tired arms. After a while he steered her across to the writing-desk.

" Sit down and send a cable to Doctor Schulze. Tell him he can start making any arrangements he thinks necessary."

The angle at which her neck was bent showed no more of her face than a cheek-bone and the patchwork of freckled skin across her nose. She was quite silent. He walked as far as the door, rejecting the weakness of emotion. She stayed as she was, head bent. " I ought to be feeling glad and I'm not. It's terrible." She turned quickly. " It's *you* I'm worrying about—not my mother. Ever since I told you why I had come, I've been asking myself the same thing over and over again. If you tell me the truth it will help. Are you borrowing this money you're going to give me ? "

He met her look steadily—echoes of a thousand lies giving his voice conviction. " You're a silly girl, Lucy. And a good one. I haven't borrowed a nickel in twenty years." His fat face wore a placid smile.

CHAPTER XI

FRIDAY P.M.

RUSSELL HEADED the beetle-shaped automobile up the avenue. The wallflowers at the front of the house were even headier in the balmy evening. He pushed the open front door, walking in to the ice-cold progression of a Brubeck piano solo. Wearing bathing-trunks, Slezak was flat on the sofa, getting the last of the sun on his reddening back. A tumbler and a gin bottle were on the floor at his side. He closed one eye as Russell inspected the room. A couple of open cans—a dirty plate—were on the bare rosewood table. Slezak's clothes draped the parchment shade of a lamp standard.

The Canadian snapped a button on the record-player. He carried the debris to the kitchen without a word. Collecting Slezak's trousers and jacket, he dropped them on their owner. "This is a respectable country house—not a beatnik's pad," he said sourly. "Get your clothes on— we've got things to talk about."

He spread out the collection of documents on the table. "Don't put a nose past the avenue gate after to-night," he instructed. "And try to remember who you are. An eccentric expatriate who can afford to say ' give or take a few thousand dollars ! ' "

Slezak slipped into trousers and shirt. He sat on the edge of the sofa, his nose in his glass. He spoke when he was ready. "You mean it's set for to-morrow ? "

Russell nodded. He pushed the collection of papers into a bureau drawer. "Don't show this stuff the first time they come. They'll know you've got it. Paul will ask if you'll sell. You say you're not over-keen but you let him persuade you. You agree on a price and he asks for an option." He spoke very slowly, making each word tell. "This is where you dig your feet in."

Slezak stretched lazily, holding his glass to the light. The white of his eyes was slightly discoloured. "Not too far, I hope—we need that dough."

"Let's cool the comedy," Russell said irritably. Slezak wasn't drunk but he'd had more than the hour of the day warranted. "You're ready to sell for cash but you won't entertain an option. Is this absolutely clear?"

"How long do I give them to find the cash?" Slezak screwed up his mouth.

The question pleased Russell. Liquor hadn't completely addled the pilot's mind. "Twenty-four hours. And make sure they understand there's no alternative!" He crossed the room, forcing friendliness into his voice. "In a couple of days you can have every dame in town lined up. What you need now is sleep. We all need sleep," he said significantly.

Slezak was grinning. "I think you're worried. You don't have to be. I'll be in there wearing my best banker's blue, word-perfect." He carried the glass and bottle to the cupboard and closed it. "And where's Lucy?" he asked idly.

Russell scowled. "How the hell should I know? Where she's supposed to be, I guess. At the Balmoral Hotel with Sergeant."

Slezak's soft whistle was an insult. "That old goat sure likes his comforts. Not that I blame him—you know, I go for that myself." His smile was taunting.

Once again, the muscles under the Canadian's jaw-line knotted till his ears hurt. "I'm going to tell you for the last time," he said deliberately. "This *is* Sergeant's daughter. You'd better remember it."

"But not your daughter! That's the angle, isn't it?" The big man leaned against the white painted wall, completely relaxed. "Good night, Sir Lancelot!" He followed Russell to the front door, standing there till the car was out of sight.

Russell took the way home slowly, indifferent to the indignant blare of overtaking motorists. He stopped at Thalwil to eat his meal at a lakeside hotel. Twenty feet below, the gently-swelling surface of the water was lurid in the sunset. He paid his bill, taking a deck-chair on the deserted terrace.

He sat in the gathering dusk, trying to shut out the tin-can yelping of a nearby dog. There was nothing he could do in the city but wait. And the waiting was worst. At least Paul was doing something. Right now, he'd be sitting across the table from Wontner. Every word and gesture the old man employed would be sapping what last resistance the other might still have to offer. A con-man was like an actor whose talent for conviction must overcome any improbability of plot. Over the past twenty years, Paul on his best day had equalled the best of them. If you thought of the racket in terms of theatre, the success of the production depended no less on the performance of the minor actors. One line fluffed by Slezak—the very first time the bum's conceit overcame his judgment and they were in deep trouble.

It was midnight by the time he was back in his hotel room. He had Sergeant on the line immediately. He let the old man talk without interruption. There was no point in relaying his own anxiety. Slezak was his responsibility. The bum would go through with it now—even if it meant standing over him with a gun. It was a pleasant picture.

Sergeant sounded tired but satisfied. " It's in the bag, Gordy! I've spent practically the whole evening knocking back Wontner's suggestions of financial help. I didn't have to ask him about to-morrow. I just said that I was driving out to see the majority stockholder. ' Why don't I come with you,' he said. ' On a deal like this you need a witness.' Are you listening, Gordy ? "

" I'm listening," the Canadian said shortly. " And what did Lucy think of all this ? "

The old man's tone was diffident. " I can only hope she didn't know what in hell we were talking about. The more I see of her, son, the more I wish she'd never go back."

" I know it." Russell's tone was dry. " We'd make a swell team. All we do is get rid of a couple of police records and start peddling Bibles from door to door. Good night." For the first time in seventy-two hours he slept without waking.

CHAPTER XII

SATURDAY A.M.

THE PILLOW Slezak had over his head only diminished the creaking rumble. There was no way of completely shutting the sound from his consciousness. He pulled his face free and ungummed each eye with an effort. The familiar room was bright with morning sunshine. He lay on his back, groping in a gin-fogged memory. He shut his eyes again, emptying the tumbler of water. It brought little relief to a parched and disgustingly-scented mouth. Scratching himself apathetically, he lowered his legs from the bed as if they belonged to somebody else.

In the kitchen, he fed coffee into the percolator, then shaved. He had no illusions about either of his confederates —they both hated his guts. That fat old fraud was sly enough to hide his resentment—Russell didn't bother. Just as soon as they felt themselves safe it would be *raus mit* Slezak.

He wiped the last of the soap from his chin. It wasn't going to *be* like that, he thought with satisfaction. He still had a couple of plays they hadn't even considered.

The rumble that had awakened him persisted. He poked his head through the bathroom window. A hundred yards away, an elderly man was trundling a wheel-barrow in the direction of the garage. It had to be the caretaker Russell had mentioned. The smell and taste of the coffee revived

Slezak. Washing down a couple of pieces of dry toast, he started to dress. Black shoes, the dark suit and a plain white shirt. He cleaned his nails carefully and brushed the short blond hair till his scalp hurt. They would see a performance they were not likely to forget. All the mystery the two con-men brought to their antics was just hoopla. You needed common sense—that and the one thing they *had* got right—larceny in your heart.

The phone came to life in the sitting-room. He took the call. The Canadian's voice was full of anxiety.

Slezak smiled. " They're on their way over—great ! I'm ready for them."

He inspected the sunlit room, flicking dust away with his handkerchief. Opening the desk top of the bureau, he littered a few papers about. Then he went out to the garden, leaving the front door wide open. The caretaker was behind the garage, forking in a pile of compost. Slezak used his hands and a few words of German. The old man produced a pair of secateurs, giving them to Slezak as if he were dealing with a mild case of lunacy.

By the time the car stopped in front of the house, Slezak was creating havoc in the rose bushes. He walked towards the two men, scowling in the fierce light.

" Do you understand English ? " he asked harshly.

Wontner's florid face was uncertain. Sergeant hobbled forward, hand outstretched. " Mr. Stanley Sears ? This is Arthur Wontner—I'm Paul Sergeant."

Slezak's nod was short of hospitable. He pointed at the massed bush of yellow tea-roses. " I'm busy. If you're from Metropolitan Life, you've wasted your trip. You want my secretary—he's gone into Zürich."

Sergeant shook his silvery head, benevolent in the sunshine. " We're here on some rather confidential business, Mr. Sears. May we go in for a moment ? " He looked at the open door.

Slezak hooked the secateurs on a bough, shouting in the direction of the garage. " Anton ! Keep those goddam maids out of the house till I tell you it's all right." The caretaker shuffled into view. He stood with his hand to his ear in an effort to make sense. As Slezak turned his back, he returned to his wheel-barrow.

The pilot led the way inside. He sat on the sofa, facing his guests. " You said business—what sort of business ? "

The old man wasted no time. " I believe that you're a stockholder in Canada Mining Union ? "

Slezak frowned. " Now wait a minute—if you've come out here to sell me more of that rubbish . . ." He got to his feet and walked the length of the room. Suddenly he stopped, his outstretched hand no more than inches from Sergeant's nose. " I'll tell you something—my father bought that stock against the advice of his brokers. Do you know what it's worth now ? " He made a sound of disgust. His head throbbed with the intensity of his acting. He looked at Sergeant, seeking for some sign of approval. The old man's eyes were blank. Slezak lowered his voice.

" I'm not interested," he said shortly. He thumbed a couple of pages of a magazine with indifference.

" You're jumping the gun, Mr. Sears," smiled Sergeant. " I'll be frank with you. We know you're in Canada Union for three-quarters of a million dollars—face-value. As you implied yourself, you couldn't raise a dollar a unit at to-day's prices. I'm ready to offer you five dollars a unit for your entire holding." His tone was reasonable rather than persuasive. He passed his cigar case to Wontner. Coughing heavily, the old man waited for his answer.

Slezak was conscious of the bald-headed man's regard. It took an effort not to return the scrutiny. " I don't need the money," he said slowly. " Maybe there's something going on I don't know about. If this stock is worth five dollars to you, it's surely worth it to me."

Sergeant's gentle headshake implied superior knowledge. " It isn't as simple as that. I've got the chance of selling to someone who happens to have precisely the same misplaced confidence as you." His plump hand balanced air. " I can make a profit of twenty-five per cent. My buyer's illusions will last exactly four more days. When his interest ends, so does mine. You and I know that Canada Union isn't worth the paper it's printed on." He scribbled a few figures on the back of an envelope. "I'm prepared to give you my cheque for five thousand dollars against fifty thousand for a twenty-four hour option, Mr. Sears."

Slezak looked from one to the other. The hell with Russell's instructions—he had to know where he was. He put the question to Wontner deliberately. "And you, sir—what's your position in this affair. You'll understand I like to know who I'm dealing with."

Wontner cleared his throat importantly. "You'll find my credit rating's as good in Zürich as it is in New York. Mr. Sergeant doesn't need my guarantee—but if he wanted it he could have it!"

Slezak resolved to play the end of the act to the hilt. He ushered the two men into the garden, ignoring Sergeant's frantic elbow. The pilot walked as far as the car with them. "I've got to get back to my flowers," he said quietly. "Mr. Sergeant—I don't even care why you want my stock. I'll sell at the figure you offer. But the terms are strictly cash. There'll be no option—no percentage." He closed the door firmly. "I don't like cluttering my head with a thing like this for too long. My secretary will get the stock from my bank this afternoon. You have till to-morrow evening to make your decision. Good day." Walking away from the car without turning his head, he pushed his way into the heart of the rose bushes.

It was a quarter-hour before he went back into the house. The butt of Sergeant's cigar still burned in the ash-tray. Slezak threw a switch, rolling back the long window. He plumped each dented cushion meticulously before going into the bedroom. Hanging his clothes ready for instant use, he slipped into his bathing-trunks. Fresh air and excitement had cleared his head and stomach of nausea. He was ready to eat.

He stood barefooted in the kitchen—milk, bread and a can of corned beef in front of him. Propped against the side of the refrigerator was a map of the canton. The Zürichsee extended like a thin leg thrust out from the knee. Three miles obliquely across the lake was the town of Rapperswil.

It was reached from the south side of the lake by a causeway carrying the railroad from a promontory no more than a mile or so away. Once in Rapperswil, there were rail connections north, east and west. Munching steadily, he weighed the advantage of boarding a train at the nearby village. The station there would be no more than a halt. Anyone taking the train there would be remembered. But Rapperswil was a junction with traffic in and out all day. At this time of the year, the coaches would be crowded with holidaymakers.

He pitched the remains of his meal into the garbage can and went out to the garden. A couple of times he shouted without response. The caretaker seemed to have gone. The boat-house was cool after the hot sun on his back. He lowered himself to the afterdeck of the cabin-cruiser and unrolled the canvas shroud. A St. Christopher medal hung from the key in the ignition switch. A disk glowed red as he turned the key. The needle on the fuel gauge showed a tank a third full. The controls were familiar. He pressed the starter. The noise of the powerful motor was ear-splitting in the confined space. He throttled down till the boat was completely steady at her moorings. This craft would do forty miles an hour. It would take no more than minutes to cross the lake. He cut the motor and climbed to the platform, carrying the boat's cover. For a while he stood there, surveying the garden from the boat-house window. No one was in sight—the only sign of disturbance came from behind the boat-house where a few swans honked discordantly.

He was whistling as he came out. There was a red brick wall at the end of the fruit garden. He spread a blanket under the peach trees and curled in a knot, naked.

He woke to the noise of tyres on the gravelled avenue. Picking up the blanket, he ran through currant bushes to the tool-shed. Using the window ledge as a foothold, he pulled himself up to the warm brick and lay flat. Russell's Volkswagen had stopped in front of the house. Getting down, Slezak walked leisurely over the grass. Russell was inside, moving about in the rooms. Still taking his time, Slezak used the back door, walking without sound on the carpeted corridor. As he came into the sitting-room, the Canadian swung round, his upper lip twitching.

Russell was jacketless. His thin shirt clung across his chest in damp patches. He seemed better-built than Slezak remembered. The pilot padded across the room, his square head cocked aggressively.

" Well ? "

Russell dropped in a chair, tension in his tanned face easing. The grey wings of hair over his ears were dark with sweat.

" Suppose it had been Wontner back again—do you have to go round the place naked ? "

Slezak covered his loins with the blanket. " For crissakes stop acting like my grandmother ! I heard the car two hundred yards away." He sat down on the sofa, one elbow pushed through the open window. " Well—what's happened ? "

" Everything," said Russell shortly. " Wontner's making arrangements to draw thirty thousand dollars from his bank to-day. He'll come here with Paul some time before lunch to-morrow. The moment they leave the city, I'll phone you. I won't be far behind myself."

Slezak drooped heavy eyelids. " I'm just the chump beginner," he said sarcastically. " You'll have to spell it out for me. I want to know what happened—every inch of the way. When they left here there was no suggestion of Wontner putting up any money—now he's in. Why ? "

Russell bent down, opening the cupboard at his side. Knocking the cap from a bottle of tonic water, he tilted back his head. He shrugged. " You had the privilege of seeing the best player in the business at work—Paul's an artist, that's why ! If you stick a carrot under a jackass's nose, you can lead him through a pig pen." He cradled both hands behind his neck. " Paul asked Wontner for nothing. All he said was that he wouldn't be able to go through with the deal. Twenty thousand dollars he could raise—not a penny more without losing heavily on realised investments."

Slezak nodded. "So Wontner declares himself in. What's he supposed to be getting out of it?"

"Fifty per cent of the profits," said Russell.

"Thirty thousand dollars," said Slezak thoughtfully. "That splits two ways with a bang."

"*Three* ways," corrected the Canadian. "You're forgetting me."

Slezak grinned. "You rate an even split about as much as Lucy does." He was enjoying himself—this guy never failed to rise. "I have to take out a little extra for a cop called Brace—remember?"

The Canadian's eyes were steady. "Not any more you don't. The moment Wontner puts his money on that desk, the cops are going to be looking for three of us—and that's the way the loot splits."

Slezak knuckled his scalp, feigning bewilderment. "Everybody else kids around yet if I do it, I'm taken seriously. You come charging out here like a constipated sergeant-major. No pat on the shoulder for Slezak—hell, no, give him a hard time!"

Russell stood at the door. "We always save the applause till the money's in our pockets. If I were you I'd remember that. I'll be here as soon as they've gone to-morrow morning. We'll cut up the dough then. After that you're on your own—is that understood?"

"That's understood." Slezak waited at the door still wrapped in his blanket. Once the gate had banged at the end of the avenue, he went inside and dialled the Balmoral Hotel.

"I'd like to talk to Miss Lucy Sergeant," he said. "Never mind the name—this is an urgent and personal matter."

CHAPTER XIII

SATURDAY P.M.

LUCY SAT DOWN to write the letter to Doctor Schulze, at ease about her father. There would be so many things to take care of—she'd have to find a room near the clinic—something would have to be done about the house. It would all have been so much easier had her father been there with her.

She sealed the envelope briskly, rejecting the impracticability of the idea. She had grown up to accept her parents' separation without question. Only recently had she come to think of them as a man and a woman once caught in a violence of emotion beyond her experience. A passion that must have flared briefly and ended in mutual apathy. Whatever bond had been between them was irretrievably broken. For as long as she could remember, her mother had spoken of Sergeant with a sort of tolerant foreboding. Accepting each cheque—each promise—as a gauge against Sergeant's future defection. Yet since she'd been in Europe, Lucy found new certainty in her father's help and understanding.

She was finishing the letter to her mother when the phone rang. It had to be her father. She'd seen nothing of him since he'd left after breakfast that morning to meet Wontner. She lifted the receiver.

The quiet voice was vaguely familiar. " Lucy ? I want you to listen carefully. If you don't do exactly as I tell you, you're going to be in a lot of trouble. Take a cab and come out to Freienbach." The name was spelled twice. " A mile out of the village, you'll see a white gate on your left. Get the driver to turn in there. Make it fast—I'll be waiting."

She listened as though involved in some radio melodrama

without knowing the plot. The pitch of her voice was completely unreal. " Who *is* this ? "

The man's laugh was throaty. " Stan Slezak. If that means nothing—you'll know soon enough when you get here ! "

The name was a link with the past that she tried desperately to establish. Suddenly she had it—the man they had met in the café on the Champs-Élysées. She remembered her instant feeling of fear and dislike—Russell's cautious hostility. She tried to speak with assurance.

" I'm not sure I understand you, Mr. Slezak. What exactly is it that you want ? "

Slezak's voice was quite pleasant. " Just you be a sensible girl, Lucy. Do precisely what I've told you or Sergeant's going to be in serious trouble. And, Lucy, I do mean serious. You wouldn't want that, would you ? "

She whispered desperate uncertainty. " No—no ! "

" Then get in that cab and keep your mouth shut ! " The phone went dead.

She sat on her bed, seeing her shaking hands without understanding. She took the instrument on impulse, pumping the call mechanism till the operator answered. She made an effort at composure. " Give me my father's room, quickly. 102."

There was no reply to the bell's insistence. She took a light coat and her purse and hurried downstairs. Somehow she prevented herself from running across the hall. The porter was helpful but slow. It was several minutes before a cab drew in front of the hotel entrance.

The porter handed her in, his stolid face curious. "Freienbach—this is a long way, Miss Sergeant." He had a word with the driver. " It will cost sixty or seventy francs."

She waved him aside impatiently. " Tell him it's a mile out of the village—a white gate—and tell him to hurry ! "

A couple of times as he drove, the chauffeur tried his sketchy English on her. She answered mechanically, indifferent to his questions. Behind Slezak's awful affability she sensed the seriousness of a threat to her father. She kept coming back to the same scene—the Paris café, crowded in the afternoon sun. The stillness at their table as Slezak had neared it. Arrogant and heavy-lidded he'd stood looking down on them. And her father had been afraid. Intuition provided her with the key—it had to be blackmail. Possibly something to do with a woman. Yet the thought of her father involved with the type of woman it must be was ridiculous.

The driver was out of the car, unlatching a white gate in a stone wall. They drove on a few hundred yards to a low timbered house. The man she remembered was waiting before the door. Big, blond and smiling. He made a move to pay off the driver.

She ran forward, catching her heels in the gravel in her haste. "No, wait! I want you to wait here—do you understand?"

The chauffeur looked from one to the other. "Wait?" he said finally. "*Bestimmt!*"

Slezak's wide grin showed the gold at the corners of his mouth. "It's a big place—take a walk round," he said to the driver casually. Square fingers found Lucy's elbow. "Come on in," he invited. He shut the door firmly behind them.

It was a big sunny room. Through the open window, dark green water lapped at a boat-house beyond larch-edged lawns.

She sat down on the sofa, as far away from Slezak as she could. He busied himself with a tray of drinks, humming softly. "Now, Lucy, what'll it be?" His look started at her ankles and travelled up slowly.

She lit a cigarette, nervously avoiding the hooded eyes. "I don't want *anything*," she said flatly. "Only to know why you've brought me here!"

He came across the room, both hands outstretched. Before she could twist her face away, his full mouth was clamped on hers. Her body tensed with fear. A stubbled patch of chin was being pressed hard into her neck.

"This is one of the reasons," Slezak said softly.

There was a sweet reek of gin in her nostrils. She tried wrestling her arms free of his powerful grip. "Let me go —*will* you let me go!" The last fragment of her cry echoed in the still garden.

His hands fumbled at her clothing. He was breathing heavily, his mouth wide in a snarl. "Come off it! I can give you a better time than that old goat can!"

She let herself go suddenly limp. As his grip relaxed momentarily, she dug her heel into his shin bone and dragged it down. His mouth gaped in agony. In that second, she freed herself, running towards the closed front door.

His voice stopped her. "Come back here, you little crook!" He loped over and stood with his back to the door. "All right," he said ponderously. "I can wait. But you and I are going to talk."

She retreated to the sofa. More impelling than her bewilderment—was the thought of the open window. He stayed where he was, his eyes mocking. "Suppose you and I level. I'm not the sucker you've been told about. Sure—that pair of bastards took the dough from me in London but it's different now. I'm a fully paid-up member." He poured himself a full tumbler, dropping the ice-cubes in with care. He looked up. "Let's make sense to one another. The London cops are still looking for Russell and Sergeant. All I've got to do is say the word and they're both behind bars." He lifted his glass in salute.

She had a feeling of shock and unreality. Yet evil certainty persisted through her incomprehension. Outside was the drowsy peace of the garden. Fifty yards away, the cab-driver bent over a flower bush, wagging his head knowledgeably. If she called, he must hear her.

"Well, Lucy?" Slezak came nearer. He hid a yawn with his glass.

She looked at him, fascinated and repelled by the way the hair grew thick to the second knuckles of his blunt fingers. Her voice was hardly to be heard. "I don't believe you!"

He sat down—the inside of his arm hot on her neck. "I like you," he said softly. "You and I can have a lot of fun. Now quit stalling, Lucy. You want to help Sergeant, don't you ?"

She heard her own voice answer, strangely remote.

"Don't you believe he's my father ?"

"I don't give a goddam *who* he is," said Slezak wearily. "If you won't use your head, he's going to be lining up for his breakfast with the rest of the cons." He circled her wrist with thumb and forefinger. "Don't get the wrong ideas about me—I don't scare and I don't bluff ! "

She knew she must concentrate on getting out of this house. "I think I'll have that drink," she decided suddenly. She took the glass he gave her. "You still haven't said what you want from me."

"Haven't I ? " She flushed under the lazy smile. "It's simple enough. You probably had other ideas but every penny of Wontner's thirty thousand dollars is staying right here." He started to walk the length of the room, his voice gathering assurance. "You can buy a lot of fun with that kind of money. I'm giving you the chance of sharing it. You're coming with me, Lucy ! "

As long as he didn't touch her, she would be able to control herself. Above all, she must avoid antagonising him. "You could still go to the police about them," she pointed out. "How could I be sure ? "

He leaned the small of his back against the mantel, speaking with deliberation. "You couldn't. You're a smart girl and I like you. That's all you can be sure of. Look—you're wasting your time with those bums—the big money's going to be with me. There's a town across the lake called Rapperswil. I want you to be at the main station at two o'clock to-morrow. It doesn't matter how you do it, but be there ! " His eyes were intent on her face.

"Two o'clock," she repeated mechanically. She tried for an acceptance of defeat that would satisfy him. She stood up. He made no move to stop her as she neared the door.

Suddenly his arm barred her way. His mouth came close to her ear. " Don't get any foolish ideas about outsmarting me. If you're not there to-morrow—if either Russell or Sergeant hears a word of this, you're elected Patsy. I'll have that old creep in jail so fast you won't notice him go." He lowered his arm and undid the door for her.

She hesitated for a moment then walked out to the sunshine. " There won't be any need," she said steadily. " I'll be there."

Once in the cab, she watched the wing mirror. Slezak's tiny figure stood with raised hand, distorted in the convex glass.

They'd driven a mile down the highway when the small black car pulled in front of them. Cursing, the cab-driver used a heavy foot on his brakes. Leaving the Volkswagen in the middle of the road, Russell ran back to the cab. He opened the rear door. " Get out," he ordered. He pushed a couple of bills into the driver's hand. " I said, get out ! " As Lucy's feet touched ground, he caught her elbow, forcing her towards the Volkswagen.

She shook herself free. " Take your hands off me," she said savagely. They sat in silence till the cab rounded the bend. The Canadian's thin shirt was drenched with sweat, his face implacable. " Did you enjoy your trip ? " he asked harshly. He started the motor. " For my money you could have stayed there—it's your father who's worried about you." He let in the clutch, spinning the car out, his off fender narrowly missing a motor-cyclist. Russell drove recklessly—one hand holding down the horn button.

She stared at the oncoming traffic with hot unseeing eyes. If he killed them both, what did it matter. Anything was better than the utter loneliness of disillusion. She broke suddenly—the great racking sobs tearing her body till she was exhausted.

Russell cut his speed. He drove steadily now, turning a cautious eye on her from time to time. When she was quiet again, he pulled the car to the shoulder of the road and stopped. He fished a clean handkerchief from the jacket

on the back seat and gave it to her. " It isn't the end of the
world ! " His voice held neither sympathy nor understanding.

She looked at him in disbelief. There was no misery
left—only a sense of injustice at Russell's callousness. She
steadied her voice with difficulty. " Isn't it ? A man like
that to tell me my father's a thief ! That you're both
thieves ! You'll even rob someone who was kind to me.
Don't people like you have any decency at all ? " she
demanded.

He lowered his head, adjusting the cigarette to the match
in his cupped hands. " You better tell me exactly what
Slezak said—it's important to all of us."

" You bet it is ! " She caught the note of hysteria in his
short laugh. Her recital was flat with condemnation.

He listened, his eyes above the trailing smoke betraying
nothing. " You can leave Slezak to me," he said at last.
" The important thing is—what are you going to do now ? "

She kept him waiting till she had repaired reddened eyes
and streaked lipstick. " That's the sixty-four dollar question,
isn't it ! Take the first plane back to California," she said
in a determined rush.

" And your father ? " The Canadian pitched his butt
to the road.

" What do you *expect* me to do ? " she asked bitterly.
" Thank him for letting me know what he really is ? "

The Canadian moved swiftly, imprisoning her arms by
her sides. His eyes were wide with anger. " I'll tell you
what you'll do—you'll go back there and tell him what
you've told me. When you're through—you'll thank
him, by Christ, for every chance he's taken for your lousy
hide ! "

" Will you let me go ? " she said unsteadily. " Two men
pawing me in one day is too much."

He dropped her arms as though they were poisonous.
She was suddenly more frightened than at any time alone
in the house with Slezak.

" Which do you profess to love—your father or a bunch

DONALD MACKENZIE

of moral concepts ? " Russell shook his head, whipping her with words. " Everything you are—the background that gave you the chance to be so goddam pure and moral—it all came from him ! "

She was seeing his face through a rain-washed window. Her voice was a whisper. " What can I do—tell me what I can do, Gordy ? "

He studied her for a long time before answering. The hostility was gone from his voice and eyes. " I'm wrong. You'll have to make your own decision, Lucy. But there's something you should try to understand. Right and wrong are relative terms. Paul's a thief, yes—but he's stealing to keep you—kill that impulse in him and you'll finish him ! "

She concentrated on the damp square of linen between her fingers. " I do know . . ." she started, moving her head irresolutely. " I can't think straight any more."

He pressed a finger on the starter. " Let somebody else do the thinking for you, Lucy. The hell with your mother. Paul will never ask for your loyalty. But for the first time in his life he needs it. I choose to think you'll give it to him."

His harshness angered her. " You despise anyone you think weaker than yourself, don't you. You wouldn't know what pity is and I'm sorry for you ! " She watched his set face. He was driving steadily, ignoring her outburst. " It's yourself you're trying to justify, isn't it ? " she demanded. " Not my father."

He kept his eyes on the traffic ahead. He answered with indifference. " Keep those high-minded sentiments for the people back in California—maybe they'll appreciate them there. Me—I've got along for thirty-seven years without 'em."

She flinched as if he had struck her across the mouth. " Of course you get along," she said quickly. " The tough Mr. Russell ! Nothing matters in life except. . . ."

His voice was savage with exasperation. " Shut up ! You talk too much. Nobody around here cares *what* you think except your father. You'd better get that straight."

She had the sudden certainty that his brutality was forced. It was as if each sought to wound the other in self-protection. She knew too that this man's opinion mattered to her, regardless of circumstance. She spoke with quick sincerity.

" I'm sorry, Gordy. I don't want to quarrel with you."

He kept his gaze in front of him, touching her knee with one hand. He ground the words out as though he had to divorce the statement from sentiment. " I love you, Lucy. And God help the pair of us."

She held his hand fiercely between her own—indifferent to everything but the sudden joy of possession. After a while she relinquished her grip. Her make-up was going to run and she didn't care. She wanted to shake his tanned mournful face till he repeated himself again and again. Instead, she looked at him, bright-eyed and smiling, matching his own despairing tone.

" Doesn't it help if I love you too ? "

He took a quick look at her. " Maybe," he said cautiously. " Sure—maybe it does ! "

He parked the car in front of the Balmoral Hotel and came as far as the elevator with her. The boy had the gate open. Russell was standing, his body blocking the entrance, intent on her answer.

" You'll let me tell Paul, Lucy ? And, Lucy—be kind! "

She looked down as the trellised gates travelled up. He was still standing there. She hurried along the corridor to her father's room.

CHAPTER XIV

SATURDAY P.M.

IT WAS HOT in the Volkswagen, even with the doors open. Russell was using one cigarette to light another. He watched Sergeant's window, reliving the moments on the highway. Nothing was forgotten. The whine of the small motor as he'd crashed through the gears. The stark unreasoned jealousy as he waited for Lucy to leave the house, and Slezak. The bitterness of his denunciation. All that to be followed by a tasteless confession that would have looked good in a woman's magazine. And he'd meant every word of it.

He'd known, the moment he'd dragged her out of the cab. Battering at the rejection on her face not only for Paul but for himself. And what happened now, he asked. This business with Wontner would go on because it couldn't be stopped. Slezak was still there—the mother—most importantly, the old man upstairs. Sergeant had no more than one chance to retain his self-respect—producing the money.

You said the word " love " he thought ironically—expecting the world to stop still and applaud. Yet all that happened was that two more people acquired a fresh set of complications.

He checked his watch. He'd been sitting there for nearly an hour. He shut up the car and went up to Sergeant's room. The old man opened the door in his shirt-sleeves. He was alone, his voice philosophical.

" Lucy's been here. Ah well, that's an end to that."

Russell threw his jacket on the bed and sat down, resting his chin on his hands. " An end to *what* ? " he demanded.

Sergeant raised stout arms. " You know as well as I do —she knows everything ! "

" She heard it the hard way," Russell said shortly. He was watching Sergeant narrowly. This was a small fat boy whose bubble had burst.

Sergeant shook his head. " It's a crazy thing to say. In a way I'm almost glad it's happened. We don't have to put on an act for her any longer. Let me tell you something she said as she left—' I wouldn't change my father for thirteen million dollars and sixteen cents ! ' " His obvious pleasure was pathetic. " If I knew what she really meant," he finished.

" Is that so tough ? " asked Russell. " Lucy's got guts and loyalty." He kept his voice steady. " I'm going to marry her, Paul ! "

Sergeant nodded. " That's great," he said absent-mindedly. He limped across to the dressing-table. He was holding a cable in his hand. " Read this—she doesn't know anything about it yet," he warned.

Russell read the typed form.

MRS SERGEANT ADMITTED FAIRFIELD HOSPITAL INFECTED BLOODCLOT STOP RESERVATIONS MADE AT MAYO

GEORGE SCHULZE M.D.

He handed back the cable without comment. " Lucy told you about Slezak ? "

The old man's mouth was hard. " She told me everything. It's too late to change plans, Gordy. Any alteration would have Wontner walking on eggs. You'll have to be out at the house earlier, that's all. Keep out of sight till we've gone. What you'll say to Slezak about this afternoon I don't know. Use your own judgment. There's no other way."

Russell stood up. " There is. I've got an idea that I can handle Slezak. I'm going out there now. What time do you see Wontner in the morning ? "

" Ten o'clock," Sergeant answered. " It's Sunday, remember—he's getting the money to-day." He gestured at the suitcase on the bed. " I've doctored up one of

Springer's certified cheques. It looks good enough for my share of the purchase price." He put a hand on Russell's shoulder. " You won't do anything stupid, Gordy ? There's no real need to let Slezak know that we're wise till the last moment." His eyes were anxious.

Russell grinned. " Are you kidding ? Slezak and I are going to have a quiet talk—that's all. Paul—about Lucy— were you listening to what I said ? "

The old man's eyes were vague. " What about her ? "

It would wait, Russell decided. " Don't let her out of your sight," he insisted.

Sergeant looked up quickly. " She'll say nothing. She told me as much ! "

Russell had the door open. " It isn't that. Maybe she needs you right now more than she's ever done."

It was black night as he drove through the village of Freienbach. A wind blew in from the lake, sending the lanterns swinging in the trees of the beer-garden. His headlights followed the curving stone wall as far as the white gate. He opened it as quietly as possible and parked the Volkswagen just inside.

Keeping to the grass verge, he trotted up the avenue. In spite of the warm wet breeze, his stomach chilled with anticipation. He'd made the promise to Sergeant, knowing that his hatred of Slezak could be purged in only one way. For his size, the pilot was lightning-fast on his feet, with the probable tricks of a man trained in violence.

Lights shone in the sitting-room and over the front door. He peered through the window. There was no sign of Slezak. The stock certificates were spread across the table together with something that looked like a map. Pushing the door open, he stood there with cocked head, listening. He called softly without response. Gradually his ears established the sound pattern of an empty house. The loud persistence of a nearby clock. The creak of timber in the wind. The sudden whirr of an electric motor in the kitchen.

He moved across the room, avoiding the window overlooking the lake. It was a map, all right. One that showed an area extending for a hundred miles north, south and east of Zürich. In the kitchen sink a couple of plates had been left to dry. He put a hand on the toasting-machine—it was still warm. Beyond the lawns through the open door, a strip of light pinpointed the boat-house. He felt his way down the grassy banks, guiding his steps towards the slapping water. The wooden bridge from shore to boat-house was slippery underfoot. Holding the handrail, he shuffled forwards as far as the window. Slezak was twenty feet below, stowing suitcases into the cabin of the cruiser.

Russell retreated cautiously till his feet touched sod. Then he ran, bent double as he skirted the patch of light from the sitting-room window. He stopped at the front door, shouting Slezak's name, cupping his hands to carry his voice against the wind. As he watched, the boat-house was plunged into darkness. It was a couple of minutes before Slezak appeared, walking swiftly from the direction of the garage. He was flushed and breathing heavily. Green slime daubed the back of his shirt.

Inside the house, he blocked Russell's view with his body, straightening the papers on the table. When he stepped aside, the map was no longer to be seen. He knuckled the blond stubble on top of his square head, his face without welcome.

" Ten o'clock at night and you come here bawling my name all over the place," he said ungraciously. " I thought you were going to phone ? "

Russell was unable to take his eyes off the blunt hairy hands that had mauled Lucy. " That's right—I was." The last shrivel of fear was gone—replaced now by thudding expectancy. He spoke on impulse. " Are you planning a trip ? "

The big man's shoulders still heaved from exertion. He turned his back, his voice muffled in the cupboard as he sought a bottle of wine, glasses. " How do you mean, a trip ? "

Russell wet his lips. He'd spoken without thinking. It was too late now to undo the brash stupidity of the statement.

" I saw you putting your bags in the boat. Doesn't that mean you're going somewhere ? "

Slezak poured red wine into a glass and set the bottle on the table. He walked round, balancing on the balls of his feet. He stopped, heavy-lidded and hostile, inches from the Canadian.

" Why can't you keep out of my hair ? " he asked deliberately. " Let me remind you of something you said—after to-morrow morning I'm on my own. Well, I'm making my own arrangements for transport." He tipped his head back swallowing the wine in a single draught. He wiped his mouth on his hand. " What's the matter—don't you like the idea ? "

Russell moved a little out of reach. The man was both quick-witted and dangerous. It needed cunning rather than force to deal with him—but it was too late for any alternative.

" I've got news for you," Russell said steadily. " You'll be going alone. Lucy's not coming." He saw the long pectoral muscles flex in the other man's chest.

It was Slezak who broke the silence. He was grinning with one side of his face, his eyes closed as if in appreciation of some secret ribaldry. " Ahah ! And what did the golden girl tell you about her visit ? "

Russell stole a few inches more ground. The only issue between Slezak and him now was Lucy. The rest was forgotten.

" Suppose *you* tell me," he invited. Skin crawling, he waited for the sign that must presage the coming explosion.

Slezak balled his shoulders, his eyes flickering.

" I was going to tell you when you phoned—this is a tramp you're travelling around with. My advice is—ditch her ! She came out here with a proposition that we split the dough two ways. The pair of us." He jerked his head towards the bedroom, wrapping the outrage in a leer. " She had another proposition that went with the first ! "

" You stinking lying bastard," Russell said evenly. His hand made a bulge in his empty pocket. " Give me the truth or I'll blow your head off ! " He watched Slezak's grip close on the neck of the bottle. Russell moved fractionally faster. He jabbed hard at the pilot's eyes, the first and second fingers of his right hand forked. He felt them sink in the puffy folds.

Time seemed suspended as Slezak staggered, clawing at his face. The bottle had fallen from his grasp to spill red across the documents on the table. Gasping with pain, Slezak stumbled towards the Canadian, swinging blindly with heavy arms.

Russell eluded him, putting the weight of his shoulder into a right hook that landed on the pilot's mouth. Again and again he pumped in blows that had Slezak sagging at the knees. Somehow the big man stayed erect, blood streaming from nose and mouth. Lunging forward, Slezak managed to get a hold on Russell's middle. Straining with effort, he lifted the Canadian up then smashed him down on the table.

Russell felt the crack of breaking wood as he landed. He fell to the carpet in a welter of glass, wine and sodden paper. Rolling to one side, he hauled himself up. They fought now with animal cruelty, the grunted fury of their blows punctuating their sobbing breathing. Slezak's face was a bloody bruise. He spat out broken bridgework, peering uncertainly. Russell made one last demand on flagging muscles, driving his right fist with all his force at a point high on Slezak's jaw. The pilot crumpled, taking his weight first on his knees. He knelt, his voice no more than a grotesque mumble.

Russell stepped back, gulping in air painfully. His hands were bleeding from glass splinters. A lump had started to grow above his ear. " Get up ! " he whispered. " Get up, you bastard ! "

The big man crawled to his feet as Russell stood the broken table on its legs. The Canadian retrieved the soggy mass of papers mechanically. The implications crowded his head as he watched Slezak slump on the sofa. A few hours and Wontner would be here and this man had to face him. Russell stuffed the soiled documents into an envelope.

There were no replacements. He had no more ideas—no strength to think. He only knew he must get back to Sergeant as quickly as possible. He walked across the room, trying to control his voice.

"We're still going through with this," he said savagely. "Do you hear me, Slezak! We're going through with it! I'll be out here at nine in the morning."

The pilot's eyes were hostile slits in puffy flesh. "Get out!" he croaked. "Sooner or later, I'll catch up with you, Russell!" His voice rose to a cracked scream.

"I'll take a chance on it," Russell said heavily.

Back at the car, he used the jerrican of water to clean the worst of the cuts on his hands. His jacket hid most of his tattered shirt. He drove flat out towards the city, stopping once at a gas-station to phone Sergeant. It was past midnight when he pulled up in front of the Balmoral Hotel.

Sergeant had left the door to his bedroom open. He sat in a chair by the window, a forgotten cigar hanging from the corner of his mouth. He limped across the room, his eyes quick with alarm.

Russell shut the door with his foot. This moment had haunted him ever since he'd left the house by the lake. There was no easy way out—no glib formula that would excuse his actions. He held the envelope by the end, tipping its contents on the bed. The share certificates were a soggy mass on the bedcover. He was unable to meet Sergeant's concern.

"Slezak's in bad shape," he said heavily. "I'm sorry, Paul."

The old man made no answer. Pushing Russell in front of him into the bathroom, he busied himself with a sponge and water. He worked on the Canadian's bruised head and cut hands till he was satisfied. This done, he found a clean shirt and gave it to Russell. Sergeant sat down again, relighting the dead cigar.

"What happened, Gordy?" he asked gently. "Give it to me from the beginning." He listened from a cloud of smoke, hearing the account without a word of censure.

When it was done, he looked up. " It's no good blaming yourself, son. We've got to do what we can to straighten things out." He sunk flabby cheeks in his hands. " God almighty," he said heavily. " And Wontner all set to go ! "

Russell pitched his soiled shirt in the wicker-basket. If Sergeant had blasted him, it might have been easier to take. Now he could only wait, hoping that somehow Paul's experience would bail them out.

Sergeant snapped finger and thumb, his face lightening. He stood up, firing his words with conviction. " I've got it ! It's the certificates that matter—not Slezak. Listen, Gordy—the bum was riding horseback this afternoon. He fell and got dragged from the stirrup. That will satisfy Wontner. You'll have to see that Slezak gets the story right."

Russell looked at the bed, grateful for understanding.

" What about the certificates ? "

Sergeant dismissed the thought with a wave of his short arm. " I'll put a call through to Paris right away. If Springer gets a new batch of paper on the first plane out, we should have it here by the afternoon. I can hold Wontner till then."

Russell nodded, bound by the familiar spell of the other's voice. " Leave Slezak to me," he promised. " He won't make a move till he's got his hands on the loot. This time I'll make no mistakes ! "

" You better get some sleep." Sergeant came very close, holding Russell's shoulders in a firm grasp. " Lucy told me to-night. Is this on the level, Gordy ? " he asked slowly.

Russell's eyes were steady. " It's on the level, Paul. I wouldn't lie to you—I love her ! "

Sergeant let him go, his face contented. " She's only a kid but it's what she wants. Somehow we've got to make it work, Gordy."

Back at Russell's hotel, the night-clerk gave him a message with his room key. The Canadian hurried upstairs to grab the phone and ask for the Balmoral number. His foot worked nervously as the moments passed. The chatter of the girls at the switchboard downstairs was plain. He was about to ask for the number again when he recognised Lucy's voice, lazy with sleep.

"It's me—Gordy." he said quickly. "I only just got in. They gave me your message."

She spoke with drowsy indulgence. "Only just got in. I don't know that I like that—it's past one o'clock."

Her soft warmth was almost a tangible thing. It came to him that as yet he hadn't as much as kissed her. Yet somehow it made no difference. "What do you want, darling?" He used the endearment deliberately.

She laughed softly. "Only that! Just to know you're safe and still love me! Don't tell me you've changed your mind," she said quickly.

He found his voice. "I'll never change my mind. Good night!" He sat where he was till a chiming clock reminded him of the hour.

CHAPTER XV

SUNDAY A.M.

AT HALF-PAST EIGHT in the morning, the traffic on the lake-shore highway was heavy. He turned in at the familiar white gate and drove up the avenue. Not till he had left the car did he see the blank steel shutters drawn across the window embrasures. He tried the front door. It was locked. He ran round to the back of the house, trampling flower-beds in his haste. The shutters on Slezak's bedroom, the kitchen, were warm in the sun. He put an ear to the rear door. No sound came from inside. He trotted as far as the boat-house. The bags were gone from the cabin-cruiser. Someone had replaced the canvas cover.

His mouth was dry. He pounded as far as the garage then back to the house. There was no doubt of it—the place was entirely deserted—the pilot gone. Russell started his motor, spinning the car on the grass in an effort to get under way. He shut out the picture of Sergeant's face when he heard the news, bitter with self-accusation. He should never have left here last night.

He drove as quickly as he could, chancing the whistles of a dozen traffic cops. He concentrated on Slezak, trying to follow the pilot's reasoning. It was no use. In spite of the beating he had taken, Slezak still needed Wontner's money. Wherever the answer lay, it was deep in danger.

He drove straight up the hill to the Balmoral. He reached Sergeant's room by a back staircase. It seemed a long time before the door opened to his pounding. He pushed by Sergeant, fighting the hammer in his chest and ears.

" The bastard's gone ! " he said unevenly.

It was a while before the other man's silence registered. Sergeant was still unshaven though fully dressed. His voice was very quiet.

" You haven't been back to your hotel since you left this morning ? "

Russell swung round. " What the hell's going on, Paul ? I tell you Slezak's pulled out. Gone ! The place is empty." He caught the old man's arm with quick anxiety. " There's nothing wrong with Lucy, is there ? " he demanded.

Sergeant's face was completely without emotion. He shook his head. " I left a message at your hotel. Lucy's mother died under the anæsthetic yesterday. I got the cable an hour ago. I must have just missed you. Lucy doesn't know yet."

For a moment the words were without impact. Then Russell sat down heavily on the bed. " Dead ? " he repeated incredulously. He wanted to laugh. The whole crazy structure was collapsing on their heads. " Jesus, God—all this for nothing ! "

Sergeant answered stolidly. " We're getting out, Gordy, just as fast as we can." He pointed at the bags behind the door. " You'd better go and pack."

" How about Slezak ? " asked Russell.   The memory of
the man's bloodshot hostility was persistent.

" If he's gone, maybe it's a way out.   In any case, there's
nothing more we can do."   For the first time, the old man
seemed happy to accept defeat.   " I want you to tell Lucy,
son.   Will you do that ? "

Russell nodded.   Both men started as the phone by the
bed came to life.   Sergeant took the call—he had one
hand over the mouthpiece.   " It's Wontner—he's downstairs
and wants to see me right away.   I'd better go down."

Russell's mind was working fast.   Sergeant's collapse
seemed to have given the Canadian fresh resources. "Where's
Lucy ? " he asked quickly.

Sergeant shrugged. " I don't know.   In her room, maybe.
Downstairs, I don't know."

" Have them send Wontner up here," Russell decided.
" You can't risk a scene downstairs.   Lucy might be there.
I'll go in the bathroom."

Sergeant put the phone down.   He moved apathetically,
chicken-necked and old.   " What'll I tell Wontner ? "

Russell chose his words, stinging the other to decision.

" How the hell should I know !   You got us all into this
mess—now get us out of it ! "   He shut the door firmly and
put his ear to the crack.

There was a mumbled interchange as Wontner entered
the room.   Then came Sergeant's voice, rich with regret.

" I'm afraid I've got bad news, Arthur.   I had a call from
Sears a moment ago.   The deal's off."

There was no answer.   Russell bent down at the keyhole.
The two men were standing over by the window.   He
watched Wontner's drooping mouth.   " Off ! " repeated
Wontner.   " How can that be ?   It's only a few hours ago
that he offered the stock for cash."

Sergeant shrugged.   " All I know is what he said.   He's
not exactly communicative.   Maybe he's heard something
—I dunno.   ' I've changed my mind,' he said.   It's as
simple as that."

Wontner had moved out of view but the scepticism in his

voice was recognisable. " Are you trying to tell me that a man passes up fifty thousand dollars without a word of explanation ! "

Sergeant went on doggedly. " That's what I'm telling you—yes ! He's leaving for New York immediately. He didn't give me a reason for that either."

Wontner's accusation was uncompromising. " I don't believe a goddam word of it. My hunch is that you got the money you needed on better terms. Nothing more—nothing less ! "

Sergeant started to flounder denial. Russell's fingers found the door handle. There was no time to waste backing and filling with this mug. He opened the bathroom door. " Get out of here, you stupid bastard," he said savagely.

Wontner looked at him with shocked recognition. Puzzled eyes went from Russell to Sergeant and back again. Whatever he said was too low to register.

Russell stood in the doorway, his mouth thin with impatience. " Just take your dough and beat it ! " he ordered.

Wontner stood his ground, presenting the top of his shiny head as if to resist some assault with it. He spoke in a husky voice. " A confidence trick. I should have known."

" We're letting you off the hook, aren't we ! I've got an idea you're kind to old ladies. You heard what Sergeant said—the deal's off. Go on home and count your money ! "

Wontner stepped back. He spoke with curiosity rather than condemnation. " Con-men ! And you a young man —intelligent and with a good appearance—you ought to be making five times as much in industry." Shaking his head, he turned towards Sergeant. " And Lucy ? "

Russell walked between the two men. " Lucy's his daughter. She knows as much about all this as you did." He felt instinctively that this man's pride would prevent him from going to the police. Wontner had lost nothing, nor could there be any corroborated evidence of conspiracy to defraud him. Russell opened the door on the corridor.

He spoke now without irony. "Charge it off to experience."

Wontner waited hesitantly in the corridor. "I still don't get it," he said curiously.

"You don't have to," said Russell. He shut the door in the man's face.

Sergeant sounded worried. "What do you think, Gordy. Will he blow the whistle?"

Russell shook his head. "Not a chance. I'll give him a few minutes to get out of the building and go back and pack." He lit a cigarette unhurriedly. "It isn't the moment to spring this news about her mother on Lucy, Paul."

Sergeant dragged across to the bathroom. "I'd forgotten all about it. Whatever you say, Gordy. Just as long as I don't have to tell her."

Russell watched him narrowly. There was no fight in this defeated old man. No heart to take a decision.

"What money do we have left, Paul?" he asked suddenly.

Sergeant spoke from the depths of a towel. "About seventeen hundred bucks."

Russell considered. "I've got enough to settle my bill —maybe fifty dollars more. We'll have to head back for Paris, Paul—it's a springboard, at least."

Sergeant dried his face then packed the shaving-kit into a bag. "A springboard for Lucy as well?" He came across the room slowly. "Why don't you go back to Canada, Gordy? Take Lucy with you. Wontner was right—you belong on the other side of the fence."

Something in Russell shrivelled. He looked past the painful jauntiness in the other's face and managed a grin. "It won't be Canada," he said steadily. "But whatever home we make is yours. I guess there's always room for a couple of good Fuller brush salesmen." He opened the door. "C'mon, we'd better go down. The sooner you find Lucy and get out of here, the better. We'll meet in an hour's time. The railroad station—near the Swissair office." He shut the door behind them.

Russell was first out of the elevator. Across the hall was

Wontner, sitting on a sofa watching them. He stood up, flanked by a pair of strangers.

It was too late to go back. Russell's voice was quick with urgency. " Cops, Paul ! Keep quiet and let me handle it." Pushing ahead of his partner, he crossed the hall towards the waiting men.

CHAPTER XVI

SATURDAY A.M.

THE TALLER of the two detectives had a pale craggy head set off by large rimless spectacles. He bowed briefly from the neck. His English was precise, his manner courteously determined.

" Herr Sergeant ! Herr Russell ! I am Criminal Commissioner Metzger—*Polizei inspektorat.*"

Russell's eyes were on Wontner. There was scarcely time for the guy to have called in the police. Ten minutes ago, he'd been ready to hand over his money—the cops were unlikely to have come with him. The American's florid face offered no solution.

Russell matched the detective's courtesy. " Mr. Metzger —what can we do for you ? "

The detective nodded towards the deserted library. " It would be perhaps less embarrassing if we went in there ? "

They crossed the hall in a bunch. Russell was aware of the porters' and desk-clerks' growing interest. Metzger came last through the glass doors. He closed them firmly, sealing off the noise and curiosity outside. Metzger's fingers found his jacket lapels. It was the pose of a schoolmaster faced with a difficult yet intelligent audience.

He addressed Wontner. " Please answer me—do you recognise these two gentlemen, sir ? "

Wontner's inspection was cursory. " Both. It's hardly surprising—I know them."

Metzger was wanly pleased. " This I expected. I believe these men to be well-known confidence tricksters. Are you also aware of this ? "

Sergeant's face had taken on a chalky pallor. Eyes on the glass doors, he watched the hall apprehensively. Wontner made no reply.

Russell cleared his throat. " Wherever you get your information, Mr. Metzger, that's a statement I think you'll regret ! "

Light glinted on the detective's spectacles as his head bobbed. The brief movement was his only acknowledgment of Russell's outburst. He harried Wontner with earnest conviction.

" These men have succeeded in persuading you to produce thirty thousand dollars. It is my duty to tell you that the whole scheme is a swindle."

Wontner changed legs, avoiding the detective's harangue. He looked extremely uncomfortable. Stepping between the two detectives, Russell faced Wontner. His words were blunt.

" You heard the man—a confidence trick, he said. Tell him the truth—has either of us ever asked you for money ? "

Wontner's chin came up. He spoke with new-found assurance. " Your information's wrong," he told Metzger easily. " I've given neither of these men money. There's never been any suggestion of me doing so ! "

Metzger dropped his hands. He smiled as if the movement was painful. " So ! Then I shall ask you to accompany me to the *Polizei inspektorat.*"

"Look—you may be a policeman," said Wontner sturdily, " but I'm an American citizen. What's more, I pay Swiss taxes. I want a better reason than you've given yet before I move an inch."

Metzger's eyes and mouth were resigned. " I know very well who you are, Herr Wontner. Accusations have been made against these men. You were said to be the victim. You tell me no—I must accept your denial. But I am not stupid, Herr Wontner. Since ten hours I am investigating this matter. I know many things—including your visit to your bank. I shall need from you a signed disposition."

The American shrugged. Russell put out a hand. "You've got Mr. Wontner to thank for not putting yourself in a serious position," he told the detective. "Now if you'll excuse me—we've got a train to catch."

Metzger's speed belied his appearance. He had the bright steel circlet about Russell's wrist before the Canadian could retract it. The other detective clamped cuffs on Sergeant. "I arrest you both," said Metzger formally. "If we leave quietly, there will be no scandal."

They hurried through the hall to the waiting police car. The two prisoners sat behind with Metzger. The second detective drove, Wontner beside him. They dropped down the hill, over a narrow bridge to Bahnhofquai above the Limmar. This was a black stone building with ponderous ironwork on the windows.

They walked up a couple of flights of stairs—along a corridor where lights burned dimly. At the door to the end office, the driver of the car left them. Inside, Metzger pushed a chair at each of the three men. He lost none of his courtesy on home ground but seemed unwilling to waste time. He leaned across from behind his desk, pointing a bone paper-knife.

"It is better that I expose my hand, if this is the correct expression." The knife flickered from Russell to Sergeant. "I am satisfied with both your identities. The report I have had from Scotland Yard an hour ago describes you both as travelling thieves. I speak further. It is Herr Wontner's privilege to say that he must make no charge against you. But the facts are in my possession since midnight. Doctor Thaler's house on the lake—the worthless securities—the clever tale that must make Herr Wontner part with his money." He took off his spectacles, polishing each lens and holding it to the light before continuing. "You see, ours is a small country with a great concentration of wealth. It is essential that our guests are protected. Sometimes against their will!"

Russell hitched his chair a little nearer Sergeant. Sweat was glistening in the old man's hair roots—he was breathing heavily. "Open your collar, Paul," Russell said quietly. The squeal had come from Slezak—that much was obvious. Yet so far there'd been no mention of him. Either the tip had been made anonymously or Slezak was in as much trouble as they were. The alternative was that Metzger was pulling a gigantic bluff. Russell's voice was a challenge. " Now look, you've put handcuffs on us—dragged us across the city under arrest. What's the charge ? You've already heard what Mr. Wontner has to say ! "

Wontner was sitting his chair like a spectator at a play. He followed each line of dialogue, each situation, with interest, divorced from its final implicit tragedy.

Metzger was unflurried. " I am holding you under arrest at the request of the British Consulate. A statement under oath is already on its way to England. As a result of this statement, I understand that warrants will be granted for your arrest. In the course of the next few days, a representative of the British Government will make formal application in our courts for your extradition. You will be charged that you jointly robbed Herr Stanley Slezak in London of two thousand dollars and certain valuable papers."

Russell pushed hard against the floor with his feet. He stared past the grilled windows, fingering the crisscross of scabbed scratches on his hands.

Deep down, he'd known, ever since he'd found the house by the lake empty. And Paul must have known what Slezak would do. Yet they'd sat up in that hotel bedroom, each unwilling to add to the weight of the other's secret fear. Reasoning like thieves, thought Russell wryly. Rejecting the law of probability unless it operated in your favour.

Even wearing a pair of handcuffs, you sought to bar the way to a cell with fantasy. It could be the impassioned lawyer who would demonstrate the weakness of the accusation against you—the tight-mouthed judge who'd be caught in some unaccustomed urge to leniency. And when it was all over, you started counting the days, months and years to freedom, certain that this could never happen again.

Slezak's judgment had been shrewd. The tip about Wontner had assured immediate police interest. Like Russell the pilot had gambled on Wontner's dislike of publicity. With Wontner bringing no charge, Slezak was in a position to go to the British authorities with his own complaint. They'd been wrong about Slezak—it was conceit not greed that was his mainspring. The beating he'd taken at the house last night had snapped it.

Russell spoke doggedly. " You'd better have this clear in your mind, Mr. Metzger. We'll fight extradition."

Metzger hunched a shoulder. " This I expected you to say. Possibly your knowledge of international law is superior to mine. Certainly a Swiss court will require the establishment of a *prima facie* case before surrendering you. These are matters beyond my jurisdiction. However, I should remind you of something." Pale eyes glinting, he groped in a drawer. His hand came out holding a slip of blue paper. " The Royal Reserve Bank of Canada. Doctor Thaler's agents have not yet presented this cheque for payment. Is it worth their while, Herr Russell ? "

The Canadian's mouth was bitter with bile. He kept obstinate silence.

" That is as I thought," Metzger said with satisfaction. " Passing a worthless cheque is an offence, my friend. Though in this case there has been no great loss. I think that it is a matter that might be ignored—provided we were sure that you were leaving the country immediately."

" For God's sake, Gordy ! " Sergeant was out of his chair. He stood in front of Russell, his mouth dragging. " What's the good," he said hopelessly. He made an obvious effort to control himself. He leaned both hands on the desk, dignity in his plea.

" I don't suppose I have to tell you that I have a daughter. Her mother died yesterday. I'd like to see her before I go."

Metzger pressed a buzzer. There was a knock at the

door. A uniformed policeman opened it. " Fraülein Sergeant *bitte*," instructed Metzger.

She came into the room very slowly. Taking the chair Metzger offered, she sat down plucking at the lap of her blue linen dress. Her hair had been done in a hurry. Ends strayed from the velvet band. She kept her eyes on the ground as if unwilling to face any of them. With a sudden rush, she was in the old man's embrace. He fondled her awkwardly, hampered by shackled wrists. Metzger unlocked both sets of handcuffs, retreating behind his desk again. His face was impassive. " So," he said heavily.

It seemed a long time to Russell before Lucy came to him. He held her close, putting his face against the sweetness of her hair. She looked up, crying without tears.

" I'm scared, Gordy. They came to the hotel for me."

He shook his head. This was the classic piece of European police procedure. The confrontation of suspects. Slezak must have mentioned two men and a woman. Russell burst into sudden anger.

" You've got no right bringing this girl here! She can tell you nothing—she doesn't *know* anything ! "

Metzger folded his hands primly. " This is your father, Fraülein Sergeant ? "

She nodded from the refuge of Russell's arms. Metzger's voice was not unkind. " Have you perhaps friends here in Switzerland ? "

She shook her head. Russell's eyes were on Wontner. The American's face was indignant. " The girl's mother's dead ! You're arresting her father and you want to know if she's got friends ! You're goddam right she has ! " He came over to Sergeant. " I don't know *what* you're supposed to have done. The whole thing's beyond me now. But I don't intend seeing this girl suffer. Wherever they send you—if she wants to go, I'll see that she gets there."

The old man had difficulty in answering. " She's a good girl," he muttered.

The thin body in Russell's grip had strained against the

shock of Wontner's first words. He bent his mouth to her ear. Nothing he could say could help—he wanted her to have the assurance of his understanding. She struggled free, turning her set face to him.

" Is it true about my mother ? "

He nodded unwillingly. She started to laugh, leaning back and shaking with the violence of hysteria.

Metzger spoke sympathetically. " It is better that Herr Wontner takes her back to the hotel."

Russell still held Lucy. Using the flat of his hand, he slapped her cheek till the jolting blows seemed to freeze her. She stared back in bewilderment. He spoke gently, indifferent to the others in the room.

" What's happened has been for the best, Lucy. It's very important that you believe this, darling. What they do to me now doesn't matter. Maybe it gives me a better right to say I love you—will you remember that ? "

" I'll never forget it," she said unsteadily. She kissed her father and left the office without looking back.

Wontner waited in the open doorway. " Am I allowed to know where you're taking these men ? "

Metzger inclined his head. " Certainly. To Central Prison."

Wontner hesitated. " If you think a lawyer's any help . . ."

Sergeant shook his head. " Take care of her, that's all I ask—we don't need a lawyer."

Central Prison lay a few miles outside the city. Both men were stripped on arrival, searched and handed back their clothing minus personal belongings. The waiting-room, the passage that led to it—were hushed, tiled and clinical. They sat on a bench, their stolid escort just out of sight beyond the door.

Russell inched his way nearer Sergeant, dropping his voice till it was barely audible. " If we see a doctor, Paul, tell him about your hip. You might make hospital ! "

For the first time in a long while, Sergeant's baggy

cheeks produced a smile. " Are you kidding—I'm walking, aren't I ? "

" Is it one in a cell here—two—or what ? " whispered Russell.

The old man wriggled his shoulders. " They're bound to split us. If we're questioned again about this Slezak deal, we've got to have the same stories. What do we say? "

" We're not guilty," said Russell promptly. " We're not fighting extradition because we're ready to prove it in an English court. Watch it," he warned.

The guard stood in the doorway, crooking a finger at Sergeant. " *Nun—der alter! Komm' gleich!* "

It was the last time Russell saw the old man for three days. The Canadian's cell was large and ventilated by a window beyond reach. There was a bed, stool and table. In the corner, a water-closet. The door was opened six times in forty-eight hours. Two guards delivered the trays of tasteless food, collecting the remains of the previous meal. Someone had thrown a bundle of English periodicals on the bed—all of them ten years old. A couple of times, Russell made a half-hearted request for exercise and to see the Canadian Consul. Both guards reacted with the same ponderous show of understanding. But on the evening of the second day, Russell had not succeeded in passing the cell door.

He had no watch. Other than the meal-time visits, the only indication of passing time was the changing pattern of sunlight high on the ceiling. The silence of the jail was unnerving. Even with an ear to the crack in the door, nothing was to be heard. Neither ribaldry, misery nor defiance. No more than the whistle of air beyond the heavy steel plate.

He walked from the inner to the outside wall and back again. Each length of the cell he turned in the opposite direction to avoid giddiness. He had counted one hundred and seven turns when the key banged into the lock outside. The door was opened by a strange warder. He indicated that Russell should follow. Traversing a maze of steel gates, they reached a room barely furnished with a table and two chairs. The guard shut the door from the outside.

The man sitting at the table looked up over a swash-buckling nose. He wore a black alpaca jacket dusted with dandruff.

" Are you Gordon Russell ? "

Russell crossed a floor—dangerous with polish. " I'm Gordon Russell."

" I'm Coulter—your Consul here. You *are* a Canadian, I understand." He riffed through some sheets of typescript. " Well, you certainly seem to have landed yourself into one hell of a mess ! "

All the way down, Russell's hopes had been lively. Lucy had somehow managed permission to visit him. He eyed the Consul sourly.

" Suppose we let the judge decide that."

The Consul folded his hands. " The British authorities have been in touch with me. You're going into court to-morrow with the other man. The British are applying for your extradition. None of this is news, I suppose ? "

" No," Russell answered curtly.

" Do you intend opposing the order or not ? " The Consul shook the ink down in his pen and prepared to write in the file.

Russell's voice was sarcastic. " Haven't you left all this a bit late ? I asked to see you two days ago. What the hell do *you* care what I intend doing ! "

Coulter whipped off his spectacles. He had brown pebble eyes under shaggy brows. " I've got other duties besides visiting jails, Russell. If you feel you have a complaint, I'll be glad to forward it to Ottawa. I take it there's nothing you want to say to me, then ? "

Russell shook his head. " I can't think of anything. Not unless you're worried about spending Government funds for a lawyer to-morrow. You're safe. I don't need one."

Coulter gathered his papers. " You don't impress me, Russell. You're like the rest of your kind. I'd say Miss Sergeant is wasting her time with you."

Russell was suddenly uncomfortable. He had an idea of the unpleasant picture he made. A loud-mouthed thief wearing a two-day beard as if it were something to be proud of.

"I had that coming," he said slowly. "I'm sorry."

Coulter looked back along his nose, his expression dubious. "I don't know why I bother, but Miss Sergeant seems to find it important. She's leaving for London to-night with a Mr. Wontner. It's impossible for her to visit you or her father here. The police have refused permission."

Russell stood up as the other man went to the door. Coulter's attitude was understandable. It wasn't enough to stamp on other people's feet and apologise. They wanted to see where your next step landed.

"Good-bye," he said slowly. "And thanks for coming."

The next morning, the key was turned in his lock earlier than usual. The guard took him down to a wash-room where Sergeant was drinking coffee, his face already clean and shining. Russell talked fast as he shaved, ignoring the guttural admonishments of the guards.

"The Consul was here last night. Lucy's left for London with Wontner." He looked at the blade with disgust. "Everybody in the jail must have shaved with this razor!"

The old man dunked a piece of bread in the unsweetened brew. He mumbled through the soggy mess.

"Why do you think Wontner takes the trouble?"

Russell dried his face on the damp towel. "Who knows. Pity—affection for Lucy. Certainly it isn't for our sakes."

Sergeant nodded. "I blame myself for getting us into all this, Gordy. I see no way out."

Russell fingered his chin gingerly—it would have to do.

"For God's sake stop crucifying yourself, Paul! We've got a chance once we get to England. Maybe we could have some thug throw a scare into Slezak. Little Arthur would know the right man."

Sergeant looked shocked. "We can't afford to pull

anything like that. Much better try to do a deal with whoever's in charge of the case. That way we might hit lucky with a couple of years apiece."

Russell took his nose out of the coffee bowl. "A deal! With Brace for example?"

Sergeant spoke doggedly. "We don't know it'll be Brace."

One of the guards was making impatient signals. Russell put his bowl on the bench. "Slezak saw Brace—and anyway, the bastard would never let the chance go." He held out his wrists for the cuffs to be fastened.

A car was parked in the courtyard of the jail. They drove through the gates to sunlit streets, cool and clean from the early-morning hosing, to the Polizeiabteilung. In a passage at the rear of the court-house, Russell saw their suitcases stacked beyond an open door.

Metzger was there, a second man in civilian clothes with him. Metzger introduced his companion.

"This is your interpreter. Do you want to speak to him alone before you go into court?" He seemed ready to leave the room.

"There's no need for that," said Russell quickly. "All we want is to get out of the country as fast as we can. Is that clear?" he asked the interpreter.

The young man nodded earnesly. "I understand—and I shall inform the judge." He listened to Metzger's quick German, and went out.

The policeman shook his cuffs back. "I am glad we have been lucky with the Bundesbeamter. Doktor Jakob will waste no time." His pale eyes were remote behind their spectacles. "The escort from England is already here. By two o'clock you should be home."

Russell was uncertain whether or not the irony of Metzger's last words was intentional. "Do you happen to know the names of the officers who've come for us?" His voice sounded cracked and strained.

A faint smile touched Metzger's mouth—to be dismissed immediately as if he were aware of its unseemliness. "I think you already know one of them—Detective-Sergeant Brace ! "

Their stay in the court-room lasted five minutes. The judge's sole concern was whether they waived extradition rights voluntarily. Outside again, the two men were taken to their escort. The man with Brace was young, with the hard stare and jerky manner of the rookie detective.

Bouncing a little, Brace advanced to greet Metzger. He was hatless, his brown hair springing from his scalp. He wore a grey flannel suit with some improbable club tie. Russell and Sergeant ignored him, signing the papers necessary for the release of their money and property.

Metzger drove with the party as far as the airport. They were ushered through a side gate directly on to the runway. Twenty feet away, mechanics were busy on the big plane bearing Swissair markings. A jeep rolled out from the airport buildings. A uniformed officer jumped from the vehicle and saluted Metzger. The Swiss detective took the two stamped passports from his subordinate and handed them to Brace. He had two slips of paper for Russell and Sergeant.

"These are court orders," he informed them. "By their terms, you are barred from entering Switzerland for five years."

Brace shook his head at Metzger, the clean-cut thief-catcher whose concern for the fate of his quarry matched his sense of duty. "I don't think they'll be going *anywhere* for five years ! "

British handcuffs were substituted for Swiss. The party of four was first aboard the plane and seated at the rear. Russell next to Brace, the other pair immediately in front of them.

It was five minutes before the complement of passengers boarded the craft. The plane left the runway in a whine of vanishing asphalt and foreshortened buildings. The course was set for the grey-violet mountains on the far horizon. Russell was sitting against the window. He leant his forehead against the buzzing Perspex. Below, Zürich was no more than a jumble of child's bricks at the end of a blob of quicksilver.

City of promise, he thought. That's what it had been a few days ago. Now two of the four who'd invaded it so hopefully were on their way out in handcuffs. The third under the protection of the man they had sought to rob. Only Slezak was missing—the genial stranger.

Russell looked round, aware of the voice from the aisle. The crew captain was leaning over Brace, pointing at Russell's hands.

" The stewardess tells me that these two men are manacled."

Brace's grin took the captain into his confidence. " That's right," he said quietly. " We are police officers. These men are in custody."

The captain's lined brown face was adamant. " I'm sorry, sir—you will have to release them. It is an international regulation. No one may be restrained while we fly."

Brace flushed slowly. For a moment it seemed that he would ignore the pilot's demand. Suddenly he leaned across the back of the seat in front of him, whispering in his partner's ear. Russell put his hands out, holding them steady as Brace fumbled with the screw-key. Touching the peak of his cap, the captain went back to the cockpit.

Russell grinned at Brace. " If you see me go through the window—don't forget to come after me ! "

Brace moved the lever at the side of his chair, stretching himself out to full length. He folded his hands on his stomach and considered his shoes. " Don't think you're getting dealt with in a magistrate's court. You're going up the steps. I'm going to see you eat a lot of porridge before you're finished, Russell ! "

The Canadian rubbed his wrists, kneading away the marks of the steel hoops. Two years in an English jail meant sixteen months with time off for what the authorities called " steady industry and exemplary conduct." You could at least see the end of it. So could the people you left outside. But the link with a prisoner was too tenuous to last the strain of heavier sentences. That's when the tasteless charade of dwindling visits began. The unanswered letters —down to the last skeletal hopelessness of a dying affection. The bluff brutality of a bygone prison governor was not forgotten.

" I'm running a prison—not a repair shop for broken hearts. Nobody asked you to come here ! "

" Yes, a lot of porridge," repeated Brace with lazy satisfaction. " You know, you made a mistake picking up a mug like Slezak. He's poison. I don't care what mouthpiece you get—he won't shake Slezak."

Russell was silent. Brace was probably right. Any of the hotel employees' evidence against them was weak. A barman and waiter, uncertain of what they had seen, unsure of its implications. But Slezak's testimony would be different. If they attacked his character, the prosecution had the right to drag out their own previous convictions. This before the jury had even heard the whole of the evidence.

Brace's eyes were almost shut tight. " Pity about the old man's daughter. Ah well—with legs like that she'll always have somebody ready to take care of her." He whistled tonelessly for a few seconds. " From what I hear, she's already made sure of it."

Russell turned wearily. " No doubt your wife finds your conversation fascinating. But you're bending my ear. Save it for the court."

They sat the rest of the way in hostile silence.

CHAPTER XVII

WEDNESDAY P.M.

AT LONDON AIRPORT, the party was first to leave the plane. Its passage through customs was brief. Special Branch men checked the two prisoners' identities. A Flying Squad car stood ready to take them to Bow Street Police Station. There the jailer hustled them into an empty court.

Russell took a quick look at the public gallery. The only people in the room were an elderly man apparently asleep in the Press box and a black-coated lawyer resting his chin on his brief-case.

It was nearly three o'clock. The normal business of the court was long since done. This had to be a special sitting, Russell decided. The grey-haired jailer came to life as a door opened at the back of the court. He prodded Sergeant and Russell.

" Stand up ! " he said hoarsely.

The magistrate took his seat on the bench, turning a biliously speculative eye on the men in the dock. Brace hovered on the bottom step leading to the witness-box. The clerk to the court read the charges in a high neighing voice, delivering the final questions as if loathing the obligation.

" Do you plead guilty or not guilty ? "

" Not guilty," said Russell steadily. Sergeant repeated the plea.

" Siddown," whispered the jailer.

The lawyer rose with a vestigial bow. " If it please, Your Worship, I appear for the prosecution in this case."

The magistrate explored an ear with a forefinger. He spoke indifferently. " Very well, Mr. Blackham. Are the defendants represented ? "

The lawyer looked at Brace who shook his head.

"I see," said the magistrate sagely. "Go on, Mr. Blackham."

The lawyer straddled his weight on widespread legs. He had an easy confidential manner. "This is a case involving a large sum of money, Your Worship. I am offering no more than evidence of arrest at this time." He made his summons loud enough to carry as far as the street. "Detective-Sergeant Brace!" His heavy jaw lifted in sympathy with Brace's ascent to the witness-box.

The detective took the oath with practised sincerity. Name, rank and duty-base followed. He related the circumstances of the two men's arrest, his shoulders squared, his answers unfaltering.

"Have you any questions to ask the police officer?" The clerk of the court made no secret of his boredom.

"No questions," answered Russell. Sergeant sagged a little, hunching his indifference.

The lawyer collected the pink-taped brief from the desk in front of him. "I intend to call no further witnesses to-day, Your Worship. I respectfully ask for a remand in custody."

The magistrate started to rock restlessly on his bench, using the mating weave of a male pigeon.

"These men have been in custody for some days, I understand. I take it that you're not opposing bail, Mr. Blackham?"

The lawyer's face set in shocked denial. "I am, indeed, sir. I am instructed that the police are not satisfied that the retention of these men's passports will ensure their future appearance in court. There are also grounds for suspecting interference with witnesses." He craned towards the bench.

The double act never changed its material, Russell thought sourly. The next lines would be the magistrate's —fair-minded but regretful.

The justice rocked to a halt. "I think you know my views in all extradition cases, Mr. Blackham. I am always unwilling to impose additional hardship on the defendants."

The top half of the lawyer's body drooped deferentially. "As Your Worship pleases. The prosecutor in this case is not yet available. I am informed that he is due to arrive from Switzerland this afternoon."

The magistrate looked at the clock on the wall impatiently. "Then there's no reason why you shouldn't be able to continue to-morrow?"

Blackham caught Brace's nod from across the room and bowed agreement. The magistrate addressed the prisoners.

"I am going to remand you both in custody until to-morrow morning. You will be given facilities at the prison for getting in touch with your friends or legal advisers. Do you understand?"

Russell climbed to his feet. "The police have taken every penny we have. I'd like this money to be made available for our defence, sir."

Brace spoke from the shadow of the witness-box.

"It's our case that these sums form part of the money stolen, sir. I respectfully ask that they should be kept in the possession of the police."

The magistrate spread his hands. "You heard the officer, Russell. There's nothing I can do, I'm afraid."

All stood as he hurried from the court-room. The man in the Press-box put away his pencil with a yawn. The jailer's heavy hand touched the defendants. "Come on, mates. Let's have you down below."

He led the way down the echoing passage and unlocked a dim cell. "I'll put you both in together till the meat wagon comes." The door clanged, to be reopened immediately. The jailer spoke with rough kindness. "Have you got a smoke?"

Both men searched their pockets automatically.

"Not a fag end," said Russell.

The jailer glanced along the corridor. He pulled a handful of shag tobacco from a pouch, added a dozen cigarette papers and a few red-topped matches. Putting a forefinger against his pursed lips, he closed the door again.

There was only room for one man to sit in the cell. Russell rolled a couple of rough cigarettes. The strong black tobacco hit his lungs explosively. He started to walk up and down.

There was no way of telling where Lucy might be. Surely she'd have sense enough to inquire where they were from Scotland Yard. It was their only hope. As soon as she found the means, she'd come to their aid. He was sure of it. Neither of them had the price of a phone call left. And a jail-stamped letter would be too late to be of use.

He wheeled suddenly, banging the heels of his fists on the door. The sound reverberated along the passage. He heard the answering jangle of keys being fitted into the steel gate.

Sergeant looked up inquiringly. " Jesus God ! " he said mildly.

Russell ignored him. The jailer flung the door open. " There's a bell, mate," he said reprovingly. He peered into the cell till he found the button. He leaned a square thumb on it. Nothing happened.

" Did you ever see one that worked ? " asked Russell. " Will you tell Inspector Weston that I'd like a word with him ? "

The jailer's red face was alive with sudden interest. " Now I've gotcha," he said happily. " Didn't they have you in here a week or so ago on an I.D. Parade—right ? "

" Right." Russell used all his persuasion. " Look—tell the inspector I want to see him—it's important."

The jailer nodded. " Maybe it is—but you won't see him—not until to-morrow morning. Not unless you manage to get into Stamford Bridge football ground." His eyes were curious. " It was him had the parade, wasn't it. Him and Brace ? "

Russell's hope sank. Weston's sense of justice went beyond any feeling of personal dislike. Had he been here, he would have used the office phone to get news of Lucy.

" What time are we up to-morrow ? " he asked slowly.

The jailer blew out meaty cheeks. " Eleven o'clock.

And with Varley sitting, it'll *be* eleven o'clock. He don't stand being messed around. Cheer up—another quarter of an hour and you'll have a nice charrybang ride." He started to close the door.

Russell fingered the lump over his ear. It was still painful. " I've had one before," he said bitterly. " Tell the driver to drop us off at the Ritz."

It was an hour before they heard the sound of cells being unlocked. The Black Maria was parked in the yard, its back facing the exit to the cells. Four or five constables lurked about, discouraging any idea of a sudden dash for the spike-topped wall. The prisoners were loaded one at a time.

Up the steps and into the passage that ran from the rear of the vehicle as far as the driver's cab. Off the corridor, left and right, ran a series of narrow stalls with iron lattice-work in the doors at chest level.

Russell took his seat on the narrow ledge facing the front. There was no room to stand—nothing to be seen through the opaque glass in the outer wall. If you crouched—one cheek pressed against the ironwork in the door, it was just possible to catch an angled glimpse of liberty through the window over the back steps.

He braced himself as the wagon lurched forward. This drive from police-station to prison was terrifying. If you were unlucky enough to be caught in a precinct on the beginning of a collection round, it could take hours before you were released from the narrow confines. You either sat—your legs under the metal seat of the man in front of you, or hunched miserably with your eyes on the back window. There was always the urge to try to fit a locality to the glimpse of vanishing streets.

He kept his seat, considering the scratched remarks of previous occupants. These had been dug laboriously into the paintwork of the cubicle's steel lining.

Eddie Foss out of Shepherd's Bush. Six moon for belting a copper.

Across this, a critic had scrawled the words :

" *Liar! Ponce!* "

Newcastle Freddy—up before that old bastard the Lord Cheef Justice. Bound to get seven!

The last defiant scrawl was in letters six inches high.

Paddy Murphy—drunk. Up the I.R.A.

There was supposed to be an escape-hatch in the roof, operated from the cab. It didn't matter. You sat there with churning stomach, expecting each bend in the road to be followed by the splintering of glass, the grinding of shattered metal.

Someone up front had started to sing in a whining sentimental drone, the words of the song loaded with Saturday night moroseness. A couple of the passengers were shouting mutual accusations of betrayal. Across the way from Russell, somebody else was being noisily sick.

He shut his eyes, covering his ears with his hands. It was no use. Nothing could blot out the futility of the years ahead—the sordidness of a jail existence. He pictured the streets crowded with people on their way home from work. Indifferent or curious as the wagon rolled by. He'd have changed places with any of them. Blind, broke or homeless. Each one had the right to freedom.

Ah well, he thought suddenly. That consul in Zürich had been right. He was no different to the rest of them—down to the last mealy-mouthed *mea culpa's*. He opened his eyes slowly, rejecting the lash of self-criticism. It wasn't true, his mind shouted. You could make an end to all this whether you reached your decision on a jail-bound wagon or standing on a stack of bibles. The point of departure was irrelevant. Success or failure depended on strength of purpose. Whatever he did now affected the lives of two other people. Lucy and her father were a source of strength no less than an acceptance of responsibility.

He came to his feet as the wagon turned sharply to the right. It was just possible to make out the dingy avenue leading to the brick walls of Brixton Prison. The Black Maria halted for the heavy outer doors to be opened. Then the great gates beyond the courtyard. There was a shuffle of feet as a policeman started to unlock the cubicles.

He climbed down the steps into the reception wing. There were ten of them from the wagon, eyeing one another with the magpie curiosity of prisoners. A jailer with braid on his cap collected the committal orders from the escort. He checked names and warrants against his charges. The gate clanged and the wagon backed into the courtyard.

Russell looked round. This was what Metzger had meant by " home."

The warder sat down. " All right, now! Answer your names. Any of you men leave here this morning ? " A couple of them raised hands. " Go on down the passage," the warder instructed. He read on. " Gordon Russell ? " Russell stepped forward. " You're remanded to Bow Street Police Court, to-morrow morning."

The Canadian nodded. He walked to where another warder waited in front of a cubicle. Once again, the door was slammed. This was a small wooden cage with a stout meshed grille for ceiling. He raised his voice. " Paul ? "

Sergeant answered from the next cubicle. " Here. Jesus, what a ride ! "

" They don't make 'em any more comfortable, do they ? " commented Russell. " Listen—do you think they'll finish with us to-morrow ? "

" God knows," Sergeant replied. " With any luck Lucy will be there with a mouthpiece, Gordy."

" We're going to need one before we get to the Old Bailey." Russell's voice was suddenly doubtful. " What's the kid going to use for money ? " He suddenly remembered the life insurance Sergeant had always carried for the girl on her mother. There was something distasteful in the thought

of this money being used in their defence. He called hopefully. " Little Arthur or someone will send up a lawyer,
won't they, Paul ? " There was no answer.

The door was thrown open again. A warder stood there
with an orderly in prison uniform carrying a can. Russell
took the mug of greasy cocoa, the hunk of bread and slice
of margarine.

" Go on down to that desk ! " The warder had the
manner of an N.C.O.

The waiting jailer looked up as Russell approached.

" Are you a first offender, Russell ? " The Canadian
shook his head. " Age, religion and occupation ? " the
man asked.

Russell hesitated. The last question was always difficult.
He remembered the anger somebody else's frankness had
incurred on a previous occasion. The guy had answered—
" Burglar "—to be reported immediately for insolence.

" I'm a salesman," Russell replied.

" Go on through to the bath-house. When you get there,
empty your pockets of everything and give your name to the
Property Officer."

Russell halted at still another desk. He stripped, a
prisoner holding up each item of clothing for the jailer's
inspection. The officer flicked Russell's few possessions
into a canvas bag. " You've got a yellow metal watch," he
intoned. " One passport and an empty wallet." He wrote
in the large book before him.

Russell stood his ground, his naked body wrapped in a
coarse sheet. " The watch is gold," he pointed out.

The man looked up combatively. " It's yellow metal
in here ! If you're wearing your own clothes, get in that
bath and hurry yourself up ! Be ready for the Medical
Officer in five minutes."

Russell lowered himself into the water. A mark on the
inside of the tub showed the permitted nine inches depth.
A thermometer hung on the wall, ready to be used in a test
of temperature. He dried himself vigorously, dressing in
the clothes that a rat-faced orderly hung on the half-door.

Somewhere along the line, he'd forgotten the mug of cocoa and the bread. He came out of the bath-house and stood beside Sergeant.

The old man's face was pink from the steamy heat. His voice was happy. " I watched the scales when that hack weighed me—you know something—I've lost four pounds! "

Russell shook his head. " A mistake. On this grub you're going to need 'em."

Keys clattered outside the room where they waited. The iron gate from the yard was thrown open, then the inner door. A middle-aged man in civilian clothes burst in. He carried his head low and wore a stethoscope round his neck. A waxy-faced warder followed after making both gate and door secure. A small red cross on a white circle was stitched on the sleeve of his uniform.

" Stand to attention for the Medical Officer ! " he bawled. Nobody moved. Striding on, he opened a room across the way for the doctor. There was a glimpse of highly-polished linoleum, the inevitable desk on stilts, a couch.

The warder carried a sheaf of medical history folders. Part of the immutable system of identification, thought Russell. The process began with the allotment of a prison number. No detail was too trivial for record.

Scars, age, religion. Name, next-of-kin and marital status. The final composite record was a twenty-page document bearing the observations of the Prison Governor, Doctor and Chaplain.

He might have described himself anyway he pleased. Ram Bulchand, for instance—a sixty-year-old Hindu bull-fighter. Next of kin—the Duchess of Devonshire. The prison staff had to get *something* on paper, no matter how improbable. Voluntary information, even the more fanciful, acquired some degree of authenticity once it was taken down. Any cell block was likely to house a carroty-haired South Londoner calling himself a Mohammedan. Illiterates answering to names such as Aubrey St. John de Vere. Confirmed false-pretencers who bore their assumed naval or military titles through a sentence with indomitable assurance. Officialdom, thought Russell, had nature's own horror of a vacuum.

The hospital officer came to the office doorway. He clacked his teeth a couple of times before getting his order under way. " Take off your shirts! Loosen your braces or belts and get ready for the Medical Officer! "

The file shuffled forward slowly, clutching at sagging trousers. Came the Canadian's turn.

The orderly announced him. " Gordon Russell, sir."

The doctor's head came up. He had a rich Scots accent.

" Have ye any complaint to make aboot yer health, Russell ? " Without pausing for an answer, he rammed the end of his stethoscope against Russell's chest. " Breathe in slowly—don't hold yer breath—my, that's a fine sunburn ye have." All three statements ran into one. He scribbled A.1. on a card.

" Outside," hissed the orderly.

Russell stayed where he was, his manner and voice respectful. " It's about the man I'm arrested with, sir— Paul Sergeant. . . ."

The doctor raised sandy brows. " What aboot him—can he no speak for himself ? "

Russell shook his head. " I doubt if he will, sir. He's got a rheumatic hip that ought to have treatment. He's sixty-six—he wouldn't get a minute's sleep on a prison bed. I thought you might take him into hospital."

The orderly was showing signs of apoplexy. The doctor nodded pleasantly enough. " Aye," he said slowly. " Have you had any medical training yerrself, Russell ? "

The Canadian made a quick gesture of dissent.

" Then get out and mind yer own bluidy business, mon! " roared the doctor. The outburst sent the orderly into action. A hand on the small of Russell's back, he propelled him from the office.

The clock in the cell block showed eight o'clock when the batch of prisoners filed in. Each man carried a pillow-case containing two sheets, a prison issue shirt, comb, hairbrush and bible. In his hand was a small card bearing his more obvious particulars. The face side bore name, religion and date of production in court. On the back, not to be exposed, the details of his offence.

Russell glanced at his cell allocation. It was on the third tier. He climbed the staircase. The waiting warder unlocked a cell along the gallery.

" Stick your card in the door—get yourself some water then bang your door shut ! " he called. He used the heavy key on its chain like a weapon, stabbing its shank into the lock with practised aim.

There was a dusty enamel jug in the cell. Russell carried it to a dark recess along the gallery, offensive both to eyes and nose. The privacy of a single water-closet was protected by a rudimentary stable door. Beyond a partition was a sink with a tap. A second faucet was set in the wall and labelled DRINKING WATER ONLY. He rinsed the dirt from his jug, each sordid detail a lively memory. The only aid to sanitation in the cells was an earthenware chamber-pot. To-morrow morning, twenty men would be standing in this recess. Some waiting to use the solitary lavatory—others anxious to rid themselves of evil-smelling slops.

He carried the jug back to his cell and kicked shut the self-locking door. He had just made his bed when the door handle was rattled vigorously. The outside metal flap on the spy-hole moved back. Looking up, he met a dis-embodied eye beyond the disk of glass.

" All right for the night ? " shouted the warder. Russell nodded. A hand on the exterior light switch put the cell in complete darkness. Suddenly a shrill falsetto lifted from one of the lower galleries.

" Of course he's all right, you melon-headed bastard! We're *all* all right. Now either go 'ome or take those bloody hob-nailed boots off ! "

Catcalls followed the sound of the warder's progress down the iron staircase. Then all was quiet. For a while Russell stood in the darkness. He climbed on his chair, looking beyond the steel-slatted window. The prison was a quarter-mile from the traffic on the main road. Down below, the circular concrete slabs of the exercise yard glittered in the moonlight. There was an illusion of ordered peace.

Suddenly a flashlight probed the shadows at the base of the twenty-foot wall. The night patrolman trudged across to punch his time clock on a checkpoint underneath Russell's cell.

The Canadian got down quickly, moving in stockinged feet. He carried his chair from the window. In another few moments, he was between the coarse, sour-smelling sheets and asleep.

CHAPTER XVIII

THURSDAY A.M.

He awoke to the sound of hammering at his door. It was daylight. He dragged himself up reluctantly on an elbow, staring at the spy-hole.

" You're going to court this morning, aren't you ? " a voice outside inquired. " Get your kit packed up—everything you brought from Reception. See your cell's tidy and be ready to leave in a half-hour ! "

Russell started to dress. He tipped the bed on its side, draping the blankets edge to edge. Then he sat on the stool, watching a starling on the window-sill run its beak through filthy plumage. Some of the old-timers, he remembered, tamed mice, jackdaws, starlings and pigeons. He'd once seen a spider and its web protected with fury against an official demand for cleanliness.

The need to have a living dependent was strong even in jail. It could evoke unbelievable patience and self-denial in the toughest recidivist. An aspect of captivity that found no place in the reports of penal reformers.

The warder's metal heels scraped along the slate floor of the gallery. Picking up his pillow-case, Russell followed the man downstairs. As they reached the last flight, the same falsetto voice was raised in farewell.

" Go back before it's too late ! "

Every man due for production in court that day waited in the Reception Wing. Russell edged his way beside Sergeant. His partner looked spruce and clear-eyed. Facing the group of warders, Sergeant spoke from the side of his mouth. " I made hospital—spring bed and pyjamas."

Russell grunted. " They're fattening you for the kill," he whispered.

The file moved by the Property Officer's desk, each man retrieving his personal belongings. The warder glanced up at Russell. " A yellow metal watch—wallet and passport —no cash."

Russell signed the book. This was rock-bottom. Broke beyond any degree of comparison. He walked down the corridor, buckling his watch on his wrist. He turned his head as the man behind him spoke.

" Ain't you got no scratch, mate ? "

The accent was at variance with its owner's well-cut suit and old school tie. Eyeing Russell curiously, the man stuffed a sheaf of pound notes into a gold-edged wallet.

Russell shrugged. A remand prison had its caste system. Prisoners unknown to one another chose their exercise partners on the basis of appearance. With money—or visitors to furnish its equivalent—a man was spared minor inconveniences while awaiting trial. Cigarettes, food, newspapers, clean clothes. Lack of these comforts was an admission of failure.

The man's hard thin face was curious. " A Yank, ain't you ? "

" Something like it," said Russell wearily.

The cross-examination was carried to its ultimate. " What are you in for ? "

Russell was patient. " The con."

The man shook his head, satisfied with the answer. " Blimey ! I thought you blokes were always loaded." He reached in his pocket. " 'Ere—cop this couple of quid—

you'll need it." He looked away quickly, whistling through his teeth.

" Paul Sergeant and Gordon Russell—for Bow Street." A warder with gold braid on his cap checked the list. The two men walked to the open gate. Half a dozen Black Marias were parked on the gravel outside. A policeman collected the committal orders and herded the two men into a wagon.

The jolting ride seemed to take an eternity. The same beefy-cheeked jailer received them at the police court. He led them down the corridor and unlocked two cells. " You'll have to go in separate this morning, lads. Your friend the inspector's on the warpath."

Russell gave Sergeant one of the pound notes.

" Can you get us some cigarettes and a carton of coffee ? " The jailer nodded. " Might take a little time. We've got a full house this morning. All the regular customers on the booze."

Russell stopped the closing door. " Has anyone been inquiring for either of us ? "

The jailer scratched an ear. " Couldn't have been—yet. It's only nine-thirty. Courts don't open till ten. I told the inspector you was asking for him. He'll be down later. He ain't in a good mood—Chelsea got beat again yesterday." He winked and shut the door.

A half-hour elapsed before Inspector Weston shot the bolt carefully. Obviously he had no intention of being trapped in a locked cell. He shut the door behind him. "What is it, Russell. What do you want to see me about ? "

Russell got to his feet, avoiding the steady grey eyes. Memory of Weston's denunciation made him uncomfortable.

Somewhere there'll be people who gave you what decency's left in you! When you make your next haul, think of them sitting there counting it with you!

He spoke hesitantly. " I wanted to ask if there'd been any inquiries about us. We haven't had a chance to contact anyone about a lawyer." He jerked his head at the dividing wall. "Sergeant's daughter is in England. I know she'll be trying to find out where we are."

Weston put his hands behind his back, bracing his sturdy shoulders. No speck of dust marred the carefully-brushed uniform. The cell smelled of the coal tar soap he used. His West Country burr was uncompromising.

"Welcome back! I see it didn't take you long to find another customer after leaving here the other day."

Russell flushed. He owed his freedom that day to this man's fair play. The debt obliged some sort of explanation. Yet there was none he could make. Weston was still a cop —with no place for understanding in his rigid code of right and wrong.

Russell covered discomfiture with bravado. "Ah well, you'd be out of a job without people like me, Inspector! Our case is on at eleven. I want to get in touch with someone about a lawyer before then. That's my right, isn't it?"

Weston nodded his long spare head. "Aye—it's your right. It happens that there's a lawyer here to see you now." He ushered Russell into the corridor and unlocked Sergeant's cell.

A middle-aged man in banker's blue was waiting by the steel gates. Unfastening them, Weston let him through. The inspector stood in sight but out of hearing.

The lawyer carried an expensive dispatch-case and wore a flower in his lapel. "My name's Marston Hyman— Hyman and Hunt of Grosvenor Street. We've been instructed by Mr. Arthur Wontner to appear in your defence." The announcement was made with some dignity.

Sergeant only just managed to control his surprise.

"Sure—he's a friend of my daughter's. You'll have met her, Mr. Hyman?"

The lawyer shifted nearer the barred window. "I've met Miss Sergeant, yes. She and Mr. Wontner will be here at eleven." He produced a brief, donning old-fashioned pince-nez. "I've just been talking to Blackham who appears for the Crown. We're in trouble, you know—there's no earthly chance of getting this case dealt with here—you realise that. They're pressing for a committal to the Old Bailey."

Russell nodded. Though he'd guessed it all along, coming from their own side of the fence, the statement carried a deadly ring.

Hyman composed himself to further gloom. " I haven't had a chance to see the depositions. But I believe only evidence of arrest was given yesterday. I've had a word with the officer in charge of the case, too. No help there, I'm afraid. In fact, we seem to have little hope—all depends on the evidence, of course." He frowned judiciously. " We'll continue our plea of Not Guilty at this stage—we can always change it if necessary."

Russell watched him with open disapproval. All criminal lawyers had the same ability to climb aboard and take on your cause whole-heartedly. In case of victory, they stood on the bridge, smiling. Faced with defeat, they produced a nimble piece of footwork that left them—at least, standing on dry land.

" What's your idea of a sentence if we go down ? " Russell asked slowly.

Hyman hitched his plump shoulders higher. " So much depends who we come before in a higher court. Some judges are death on this type of offence—others lenient. We need strong counsel—someone skilled in a plea of mitigation. Three years apiece, I suppose. That is always accepting that they don't put a further charge of conspiracy against us." He snapped his brief-case shut.

Russell had a sudden revulsion for this useless conversation. Hyman knew better than most, how the case must end. But he'd go on producing thin echoes of hope right down to the moment of sentence. And maybe even afterwards. He had a fee to earn.

" Is it definite that Miss Sergeant's going to be here ? " Russell asked.

Hyman turned the watch on his wrist. " I saw her an hour ago—with Mr. Wontner. They should be here any minute now. Incidentally, I'll do what I can about the photographers—I know one or two of them."

Sergeant's face flushed. " What do you mean, photographers ? What in hell do they have to do with it ? "

Hyman's regret carried small conviction. " I'm afraid the reporters are on to us, Mr. Sergeant. From their point of view there couldn't be better material. There was a picture of this man Slezak in one of last night's papers. Taken in uniform—the gallant pilot, do you see ! And the rest of the story's perfect. Extradition—both of you, if I may say so, colourful figures. And behind the scenes, the good-looking girl from California. But I'll do my best ! " He walked to the gate where Weston let him through.

The inspector walked back slowly. Russell was last to be locked away. He waited in the doorway, speaking on impulse. " You think I'm a first-class creep, don't you, Inspector. Without even the decency to say thanks for what you did here the other day."

The man had the key in the lock. He lifted his head, considering Russell speculatively. " You've got nothing to thank me for. Every man who comes into this station gets what are his rights—no more—no less ! "

There was desperation in the Canadian's tone. " Just as soon as the hearing's over, there'll be a girl down here to see me. I want you to give me five minutes with her alone. Five minutes—that's all."

Weston's grey eyes were weary. He spoke quietly. " I've been at this job for twenty-four years, Russell. You're right—people like you give me my job. There's something I've learned in that time." He tapped the shank of the heavy key with a finger. " This is when you all start to think of your womenfolk. When it's too late ! " He closed the door in Russell's face.

The Canadian sat down, lighting a cigarette with nervous fingers. He had no hatred for Weston. The inspector applied his beliefs, indifferent to gratitude or hostility— somehow leaving a man his self-respect.

It was five-to-eleven when keys rattled outside the door

again. The jailer wheezed asthmatically. " Up we go—all aboard for the Skylark ! "

Both men stood at the bottom of the steps leading to the dock. Their names were called in the clerk of the court's clear tenor. They started up the stairs. In the dock, Russell turned to inspect the crowded room. The Press-box was full—every seat in the public benches occupied. Off to the left, Brace's curly head bobbed among a group of detectives. The brief movement of an arm caught Russell's attention. It was Lucy. She was hatless, her eyes hidden behind dark sun-glasses. Wontner stood beside her.

The defendants sat down. Hyman lolled at the table next to the Crown Attorney. Both lawyers were whispering, their expressions amicable. A couple of actors, thought Russell, rehearsing their lines for the big duel scene.

The magistrate leaned his weight on his forearms and inspected the solicitors' bench. Catching his eye, Hyman came to his feet.

" I appear for the defendants, Your Worship."

The magistrate smiled secretly, as if remembering an old but well-loved story. He tilted a little to his left. " You're ready, Mr. Blackham ? "

The prosecutor's voice was muted. " I find myself in some difficulty, Your Worship. I understand that my principal witness has still not arrived. With your permission, I propose calling the others first."

The magistrate's bird-like gyrations began again. He rocked to a halt. " This is all very unsatisfactory, you know, Mr. Blackham. You told me yesterday that Mr.—" he found the name on the papers in front of him—" Mr. Slezak, would definitely be here this morning." He looked sharply towards the back of the court as if to detect some further cavalier behaviour. " What *is* the position, exactly ? " he asked testily.

Brace pushed his way to the table beneath the judge's bench. He muttered something to the clerk of the court who relayed the information behind a raised hand. Somebody coughed, the sudden bark disturbing the silent room.

The magistrate nodded impatiently. "Very well, Mr. Blackham. Call your first witness. The sooner we get on the better."

Russell listened as the three hotel employees took the stand. Each one's recital was unembroidered. It was as though the Bartenders' Union had seized the occasion to bring their plight before the public. Yes, they remembered seeing the defendants on the night in question. Maybe there had been another man with them. It was hard to say. They worked long hours and were short-staffed. No witness recalled seeing a dropped wallet though there may well have been one.

The last man into the box was a complete stranger to both defendants. Small, pugnacious, he gave his evidence without hesitation. He'd been sitting in the lobby of the hotel on that evening. For want of something better to do, he'd watched the defendants. He'd seen a tall American with them—he'd been near enough to hear the man's accent. And he'd seen the interchange of wallets. This pair, he nodded at the dock, had gone out of the hotel and they never came back. He squared his shoulders ready for cross-examination.

"No questions," said Hyman.

The Crown solicitor paused respectfully. "That's as far as I'm able to go this morning, sir."

The magistrate cradled his hands. He looked from dock to solicitors' bench and back again. He spoke finally. "I intend remanding this case till four o'clock this afternoon. I shall expect you to be ready to continue then, Mr. Blackham."

Hyman stood. "If it please Your Worship, I have an application to make on behalf of Miss Sergeant. She wishes to be allowed to see the prisoners. One is her father. The other, she tells me, her fiancé."

A couple of reporters in the Press-box scribbled energetically. One man raised himself, trying to get a better look at the back of the court, where Lucy was sitting.

The magistrate assembled his papers. "This is entirely

a matter for the police, Mr. Hyman. Subject to their regulations, I have no objection."

The prisoners were barely back in the cells before Hyman arrived. Once again, they stood in the corridor, Inspector Weston a dozen yards away at the gate. Hyman lowered his voice. " Miss Sergeant is waiting to see you. But first I want to explain the position. The magistrate's anxious for this case to be finished to-day, one way or another. There's a difficulty—nobody seems to know what's happened to Mr. Slezak. The police are ringing Zürich for information. Somebody there will know what time he left."

Russell spoke quietly, controlling the quick thudding hope. " Suppose he isn't in England at all—suppose he's gone somewhere else ? "

Hyman smiled polite disbelief. " I'm afraid that's very unlikely."

Russell moved his head impatiently. This man dealt with logical progressions of thought. Never having met Slezak, Hyman was incapable of understanding the pilot's need to protect his façade. The conceit that could push him beyond reason and probability.

" What happens if Slezak doesn't get here this afternoon?" Russell asked obstinately.

Hyman pursed thin lips. " The magistrate can further remand the case or decide it on the evidence taken. This is what he *can* do—what he will do is a different matter. I wouldn't be doing my duty if I didn't advise you against building up false hope. Witnesses *don't* disappear ! "

Alone again in his cell, Russell resumed the aimless pacing. Any sort of movement was better than sitting there dead from the ankles, he thought. Hyman's professional front had been impregnable. Russell still had no idea whether the lawyer knew more about Slezak than he professed. Hyman was probably right, nevertheless. Slezak's ultimate arrival was inevitable. The alternative would be too improbable.

The click of feminine heels outside, stopped him in his tracks. The footsteps neared then passed. He heard the cell next to him being unlocked. He put an ear against the dividing wall. Lucy's voice was muffled but recognisable. Russell worked on his bell-push. This time there was immediate response. The jailer opened the door inches, pushing his head into the aperture. "Easy," he warned. "The boss is out here!"

Russell passed the end of his tongue across his lips. "Is Detective-Sergeant Brace in the building?"

"He just went out to lunch," answered the jailer.

The Canadian's face was hard. "Tell him I want to see him as soon as he gets back. It's important."

CHAPTER XIX

THURSDAY P.M.

LUCY SERGEANT watched the cell door close on her father with a sense of wonder. This place was a long way from Salinas County Court-House. There, you called the trusties who weeded the stone-flag walks—by their first names. And Ed McGuire, the jailer, was about as sinister as blueberry-pie.

She was suddenly aware of the quiet voice behind her. "I believe that you wanted to see the other prisoner, as well, Miss Sergeant?"

"I do indeed. He's my fiancé." It was the second time that day that she had used the word—deliberately yet without bitterness or defiance.

Inspector Weston led the way down the corridor. "He's asked to see you alone. I'm afraid that's impossible, miss. But I'm putting you in my office."

He held the steel gate open for her. In Weston's office, a constable sat at a desk typing. The inspector shut and locked the windows. He touched the constable's shoulder. "Go out and see what the weather's like, Fletcher. It ought to take you a half-hour." He pushed a couple of chairs to the centre of the room. " I'll get him," he told Lucy.

She stood by the window, watching the stretch of corridor. As the two men came into the room, she ran to Russell and held him fiercely close.

Weston busied himself at a filing cabinet. His back was turned to them. " You've got ten minutes," he said briefly.

She stood, lost to sense of place or time till Russell took her hands. " I don't want you to worry about Paul, Lucy," he told her. He shook her gently. " Do you hear me ? "

She avoided his eyes, unwilling for him to see her anxiety and share it. " He's old," she said hesitantly. " Will it be a long time, Gordy ? "

He answered with quiet emphasis. " There's a chance that one of us can beat this case. If they'll accept a plea of not guilty from your father, I'll plead guilty."

She looked up uncertainly, her voice a whisper. " Do you think they'll do it ? "

" That's what I'm going to find out," he answered with assurance.

She pushed her fingers into his sleeve, watching him as though she must remember every line on his face. " I think you're the best man I ever met," she said distinctly.

Russell grinned back at her. She felt his muscles harden under her finger. " I wish you'd tell that to the magistrate ! If this thing works, Lucy, it'll mean my mind will be easy— you'll be with Paul. If it doesn't . . ." he shrugged. " How long's Wontner going to stay ? "

" Not long. He has to get back. If it hadn't been for him . . ." She buried her face again on Russell's chest, determined not to give way. " Did you know he's paying for the lawyer ? It makes me feel terrible. He won't talk about you or Daddy—but he's kind, Gordy. *Kind!* "

Russell lifted her chin. " The inspector's getting jumpy, darling. We're going to have to break it up. Don't say anything to Hyman about my plan. I've got to see for myself if it's got a chance of working first."

The inspector closed the door of the filing cabinet.

"Time's up! Now if you'll wait here, miss, till I come back."

She stood at the doorway watching the two men down the corridor. As he reached the gate to the cells, Russell turned. She moved her head up and down vehemently. She was still staring, hot-eyed and tremulous, when Weston returned. He shut the door carefully. Head bent, he studied the tips of his brightly polished boots.

"I've got two daughters of my own, Miss Sergeant. I'm trying to put them in your place. Have you got any idea what you're getting yourself into? This man's a professional thief—you're not going to change a man like that."

She said what she believed. "I don't have to—he'll do that for himself!"

His grey eyes were troubled. "Anything he says, you'll accept, isn't that it? Now, if he gets your father off, he'll be a hero! You'll go and hold his hand in prison and the people who put him there will be the villains." He shook his head.

It was a different approach, she thought, but this man was as hostile as the curly-haired detective who'd come to the hotel last night. To pump her about Wontner—his interest in the case—her connection with Russell.

"I wouldn't care if he'd broken a million laws," she answered defiantly. "None of you would have the guts or decency to do what he's done."

The inspector raised both hands as if warding off her anger. His expression was bewildered. "He's robbed a man, hasn't he?" he said wearily.

Her voice was hot with accusation. "You won't even wait for a jury to decide that, will you? If he goes to prison, one person's to blame. *Me!*"

There was someone at the door. Weston held the handle firmly, his roar filling the small office. The footsteps retreated hurriedly. Lucy found the chair, gripping its sides with shaking hands. She flinched as Weston came towards her, his sombre face speculative.

"Well?" he said softly.

The first time she had told this story had been for Wontner. Repetition made it easier.

She relived the months of her mother's sickness—the last days in California. The cable to her father, her arrival in Europe.

She finished, the handkerchief in her fingers a wet ball. She felt no unhappiness, only relief. " I never understood why the law has no heart, Inspector. *We* have. And people like you and I make the law."

He went as far as the door and stood for a moment, his head bent. His voice was sombre when he at last looked up. " We make laws and we hope for justice. Good night, miss ! "

She hurried out to the street. A light summer rain had started to fall, leaving the pavement wet and greasy. Wontner sat in the hired Rolls parked before the court-house. He gave the chauffeur an instruction on seeing her. Once the heavy limousine had started towards the Strand, Wontner shut the glass division between them and the driver.

He spoke firmly yet kindly. " No tears now. We're going to lunch at the Savoy if that's all right with you. . . ."

She smiled, blinking, and groped for his arm. " Day by day you make it harder for me to be able to repay you— *ever*! "

" How were the prisoners ? " He shrugged at the sudden frigidity in her face. " For God's sake, Lucy ! The world goes on, whatever happens, honey. You'll have to realise this. Trying to shut yourself out from what's left will help nobody."

Her contrition was real. " I know—I'm being stupid and unrealistic." She focused her eyes resolutely on the chauffeur's back. " They're cheerful enough, I guess. Gordy's got an idea he may be able to get Daddy off." She frowned as though the memory bothered her. " And I've just done the craziest thing—really feminine and juvenile ! I told a uniformed inspector the whole of my story—just as I told it to you. And I still don't know why."

Wontner nodded. " What did he say ? "

She looked embarrassed. " ' We make laws and hope for justice ' ! "

Wontner tapped the glass. " That's the sort of remark that is sometimes described as philosophy. Only it has to get into print first." He opened the car door, tucked her hand under his arm and led her into the grill room.

A well-known actor and his wife were at the next table. Over against the wall, she recognised the crew-cut and pallor of a political Hollywood expatriate. At any other time, she might have surrendered to the excitement of the moment. As it was, she pecked uninterestedly at the meal Wontner had ordered. Wherever she looked, she saw Russell's face as he'd turned at the steel gates and waved.

Wontner repeated his question. " I asked you what you'd do when the trial's over, Lucy. Go back to California ? "

She answered without hesitation. " No—I'll get some sort of job here. I'll sell up what there is in California and bank the money. They're going to need it."

He wiped his mouth vigorously on his napkin. " I rather expected to hear you say that, Lucy. Well—you know where to find me if ever you need me."

She was unable to stop the quick tears. From the beginning she had been drawn to this kindly man.

" Don't you think you've done enough for us all ? " she asked quietly.

He shrugged diffidently. " I'm a selfish man. It's given me real pleasure to help you, Lucy." He made a pattern of spoon, fork and glass, destroying it as suddenly. His voice was mild. " You don't stop stealing unless you have an alternative way of making a living. I hope both your father and Russell will find one." He checked his watch. " Four o'clock, that judge said. If we go now, we've got time for a movie."

CHAPTER XX

THURSDAY P.M.

RAIN DRIFTED against the window, gurgling in the guttering overhead. Detective-Sergeant Brace wiped the top of the table fastidiously before sitting on it. He thrust head and body towards Russell like a fox scenting hounds. Here in the privacy of the cell, he made no attempt to hide his hostility.

" What do you want ? "

" A deal," said Russell quietly. " Me for the old man."

Brace's mouth slid away from his teeth, leaving a bare derisory grin. " What's that supposed to mean ? "

Russell moved out of his corner. " We're alone—let's play this in the open, Brace. You want me—not Sergeant. Maybe it won't be as easy as you think. With a good lawyer and an Old Bailey jury, we've got a fifty-fifty chance."

He ploughed on, ignoring Brace's blowing dissent. " There's nothing for us to lose by attacking Slezak's character. How long's he going to stand up under a really tough cross-examination ! "

Brace used a foot to narrow the gap in the door. " I had a word with Slezak only ten minutes ago. He won't mind a little mud-slinging. Certainly the judge won't. You're forgetting something important. The law doesn't mind *who* you steal from—the offence is still there." He eased himself to the ground, bringing his face no more than inches from the Canadian's. His eyes were implacable. " You're right, Russell. You're the one I want. Make it easy for me ! "

Neither man moved, locked in impending violence. Russell broke the silence. " If you can get Blackham to drop the charge against Sergeant, I'll plead guilty."

Brace wiped his forehead with the back of a shaking hand. His laugh echoed in the cell. " Christ, what an actor !

Now he wants to play the hero! That's for the daughter, I suppose. You're a bigger bloody fool than I thought you were." He was suddenly serious. "All right. I'll see Blackham. It's up to him. You'll plead guilty now—when we get into court—is that the idea?"

"That's the idea," repeated Russell.

Brace turned from the door. "I'll still see that you get five," he said pleasantly. He slammed the wood behind him.

Russell leaned against the wall drained of energy. Better that Sergeant heard the news in open court. By that time it would be too late for him to do anything but walk out a free man. It had been touch and go with Brace. Now that Slezak's appearance was definite, the bargain was a fair one.

He looked at his watch unnecessarily—the nervous spasms in his stomach a better indication of the approaching hour. The key was turned, the door opened again, before he realised it.

Inspector Weston came into the cell, seeming to measure his steps. He squared his shoulders, the look on his face enigmatical.

The Canadian watched curiously. Weston was no less a cop than Brace. Yet always he inspired this urge to talk to him—to justify yourself in some way. Russell had the sudden impression that the inspector was on the brink of saying something. But Weston remained silent.

Russell shrugged. "All right, Inspector, say it. Why don't I get out of Miss Sergeant's life, etc.—I'll tell you why —neither of us wants it!"

Weston's voice was quiet. "You've just told Detective-Sergeant Brace that you'll change your plea?"

Russell stared his astonishment. "What of it?"

"Does your solicitor know about it?" asked Weston.

"Not yet—does it matter?" said the Canadian.

Weston shifted feet, lifting his head. He went on with determination. "Once you plead guilty, the prosecutor's appearance is a matter of form. Slezak could be five thousand miles away and a judge could still send you to jail."

Russell stared back warily. " Only Slezak's right here, isn't he ? What *is* all this, anyway ? "

Weston's voice was rusty with strain. He came nearer Russell. " I gave Brace the message an hour ago. Slezak left Zürich for Beirut at seven o'clock this morning ! "

They climbed up to the dock, their feet scuffing the stone steps. Sergeant moved more slowly, grunting as he heaved himself on his lame hip. He grabbed at Russell's jacket. " What in hell's going on, Gordy ? Your cell's been like Grand Central Station all afternoon ! "

Russell put a palm in the small of the old man's back, hoisting him over the last three treads. Excitement made the Canadian's voice unsteady.

" Keep your eyes on Brace and get ready for a shock ! "

The court-room was crowded again—stuffy with the smell of damp clothing. A carnation glowed in a tumbler on the magistrate's bench. Brace was at the solicitors' table talking animatedly to Blackham. Both men swivelled round as the defendants entered. Hyman presented his back, busying himself with pencil and paper.

The clerk came to his feet. He whispered conspiratorially to the magistrate. The magistrate waited till the shuffle of feet and rasping coughs were stilled. The room now had the hush of a theatre as the curtain is raised.

" Mr. Blackham ! "

The magistrate's summons echoed in the corridor under the dock. The Crown solicitor stood, his expression a mixture of caginess and respect. " Your Worship, I have just been informed by Detective-Sergeant Brace that he has seen the defendant Russell since court recessed." He flung a hand at the dock, his faint smile acknowledging the Canadian's wisdom. " I understand Russell now wishes to plead guilty. In view of this, Your Worship, I am asking you to take a certain . . . "

He had no chance of finishing. Hyman was up beside him, flushed and expostulating.

" I know nothing at all about this ! "

Russell wet his mouth, sitting hard into the rough bench,

locking his fingers on its edge. The whole court seemed to grow smaller, ringing him with a hundred expectant faces. He concentrated on the flower in the glass before the magistrate. He spoke deliberately.

"Detective-Sergeant Brace misunderstood me. My plea is not guilty!"

Brace's face was shocked. His full mouth struggled for an answer. For a moment it seemed as if he would rush at the railed dock. Blackham put out a restraining arm. Hyman sank down, his face still red with indignation.

The Crown solicitor's voice was barely audible. "I must apologise, Your Worship. I call no further evidence. The prosecutor in this case is not available." He ducked his head, dissociating himself from the detective beside him.

Hyman rose. "I ask for this case to be dismissed, Your Worship. From beginning to end, my clients have maintained their innocence in face of a prosecution that has been shown to be unwarranted. I have no doubt whatsoever that you will see fit to grant an order for costs against the police." He leaned back confidently.

Somewhere at the back of the court, a constable called for silence. The magistrate's fingers were flicking the pages on his blotter. Lifting his head as if listening, he wrote for fully a minute before giving judgment. He considered the men in the dock.

"What I have to say concerns everyone in this case. Someone has deliberately wasted the time of the court. I suspect both of you men might know the reasons for this far better than I do. I am discharging you both. However, I make no order as to costs." Hard shrewd eyes found Brace. "I want all the papers in this case assembled, Detective-Sergeant. I shall send them to the Commissioner of Police with my personal comments. Making a farce of criminal proceedings can be a dangerous form of amusement." He bowed to the room and left the bench.

Vaguely, the Canadian knew that the jailer was talking to him. A steady drum in his ears made it impossible to hear. He got to his feet with an effort, following Sergeant down the stairs leading to the well of the court. They pushed their way through the ring of curious faces, indifferent to the meaningless babble of well-wishers.

There was no sign of Lucy. Beyond the heavy open doors of the lobby was the street. Outside, a Covent Garden porter passed by, a swaying tower of baskets on his head. A couple of draught horses stood in the rain, their wet hides steaming. Then even as Russell watched, he saw Lucy hurrying up the steps.

Sergeant's voice held quiet assurance. " Nothing's ever going to look as good again, Gordy."

Russell took a deep breath. " Nothing," he said happily. Smiling, he walked towards the girl who was waiting.

>>> If you've enjoyed this book and would like to discover more great vintage crime and thriller titles, as well as the most exciting crime and thriller authors writing today, visit: >>>

The Murder Room
Where Criminal Minds Meet

themurderroom.com

www.ingramcontent.com/pod-product-compliance
Ingram Content Group UK Ltd.
Pitfield, Milton Keynes, MK11 3LW, UK
UKHW022313280225
455674UK00004B/284